BRED BY THE SLUMS

Lock Down Publications and Ca$h
Presents
Bred by the Slums
A Novel by *Ghost*

Lock Down Publications
P.O. Box 870494
Mesquite, Tx 75187

Lock Down Publications
Like our page on Facebook: Lock Down Publications @
www.facebook.com/lockdownpublications.ldp
Cover design and layout by: **Dynasty Cover Me**
Book interior design by: **Shawn Walker**
Edited by: **Sunny Giovanni**

Stay Connected with Us!

Text **LOCKDOWN** to 22828 to stay up-to-date with new releases, sneak peaks, contests and more…

Thank you!

Submission Guideline.

Submit the first three chapters of your completed manuscript to ldpsubmissions@gmail.com, subject line: Your book's title. The manuscript must be in a .doc file and sent as an attachment. Document should be in Times New Roman, double spaced and in size 12 font. Also, provide your synopsis and full contact information. If sending multiple submissions, they must each be in a separate email.

Have a story but no way to send it electronically? You can still submit to LDP/Ca$h Presents. Send in the first three chapters, written or typed, of your completed manuscript to:

LDP: Submissions Dept
Po Box 870494
Mesquite, Tx 75187

DO NOT send original manuscript. Must be a duplicate.

Provide your synopsis and a cover letter containing your full contact information.

Thanks for considering LDP and Ca$h Presents.

DEDICATION

This book is dedicated to my precious, beautiful
Babygirl. The love of my life, 3/10. Everything I do
is for YOU, first and foremost.

ACKNOWLEDGEMENTS

I would like to thank the Boss Man and C.E.O of
LDP, Cash. Thank you for this opportunity. Your
wisdom, motivation and encouragement are
appreciated. Thanks, Bruh.

To the Queen and C.O.O of LDP, thank you for all
that you do Sis. Your hard work, dedication and
loyalty to this company never goes unnoticed.

Ghost

Chapter 1

As soon as I heard the front door to the house close, and the ignition of the Pastor's Mercedes Benz turn over, I finished gargling the Scope in my mouth and spat it out into the sink before running the water, so it would wash it all down the drain. I knew that Sister Jones would be knocking on my door at any minute, especially since her daughter was sleeping over at one of her friend's houses. I knew she wouldn't be able to stay away from me.

I wiped my mouth on my face towel, and just as I was putting it back on the hook, I heard the knock on my bedroom door, before it opened. I took a deep breath and stepped into my room, and there she was. All five feet, three inches of her. Light skinned, with freckles that decorated her soft cheeks. Sholder-length, naturally curly hair that she kept from graying by dying it every other week.

She was dressed in a purple negligee that barely covered her thick thighs. Her breasts were about a strong C-cup, her stomach flat, and behind her was an ass that still made men eye it until it disappeared from their sight. She was built like a southern goddess, and no man could deny that fact.

She approached me slowly, stopping right before she was close enough to touch me. "Son, I know I said that I wasn't gon' be all over you for a few weeks, but it's just…" She fidgeted with her fingers. "I need you. My *body* needs you. You know how crazy that man makes me, Shemar, and you're the *only* one that can heal me." She stepped forward, runningher hands across my well-developed chest.

Even though I was only seventeen years old I was more than conscious of my body, and I wanted to make sure that I always presented my best possible self.

I opened my arms, allowing her to step into them. My senses heightened as I inhaled her intoxicating perfume, Woman by Ralph Lauren. That, paired with her natural scents, caused me to feel some type of way.

She kissed my chest and ground her pelvis into me, moaning at the back of her throat, while I wrapped my arms around her waist and enjoyed the scent coming from her scalp. One of the many perks I enjoyed, being that I towered over her at 5'9.

"Baby, make love to me before he gets back. I need all of this in me. My body craves it." She reached between us, sliding her hands into my boxers, squeezing my dick, before running her thumb along my head.

That always drove me crazy and made me feen for her even more. She kissed my neck, then bit it hard. "You want some of yo' momma, baby? Huh? Do you still desire me? Am I the only one that still drives you crazy?" she asked, pulling my boxers all the way down, sinking to her knees.

I felt her squeeze my dick again, as she began stroking it, before kissing the head, looking up at me, waiting on a response I assumed. She squeezed it tighter.

I moaned. "Yeah, I want you, momma. You know you drive me crazy. Only you do."

She slid me into her mouth and slipped her arms out of her negligee, exposing her round, yellow titties with her big, beautiful brown nipples that stood erect. She started to suck me loudly, and the noises started getting to me right away. That, and the way her titties were bouncing and knocking into each other.

I loved older women. I loved the way their bodies were made, and how they got down behind closed doors, and it was all because of her. She had gotten me addicted to her body at the tender age of thirteen, four years after her and her husband adopted me.

I wrapped my hand into her hair and guided her face back and forth on my penis. The noises were getting louder and louder.

She popped him out and ran him along her cheek, looking up at me. "Shemar, I still can't believe how big this thing is. It's like you were meant for momma." She kissed the head, sucked it back into her mouth, then stood up and pulled me toward the bed. She back-pedaled, sucking on her bottom lip, looking at me real seductive like.

The only light in the room came from a lamp on the side of my bed. I watched her back all the way up until she was sitting on the bed, pulling her negligee up, exposing her trimmed pussy. She lifted her feet and sat them on the bed beside her, causing her pussy to be on full display, before separating her thick sex lips with her pointy finger. At seeing that, my dick got super hard. I loved when she touched herself in front of me. I loved watching how her kitty opened up to reveal its pink, and then her scent really drove me over the edge. She was the first female to teach me how to eat pussy. I got addicted to her scent, because every day before school, she used to slide two fingers into herself before putting them up my nose and rubbing her juices into the hairs in there. So, all throughout the day in school, all I could smell was her.

I dropped to my knees and pulled her all the way to the edge of the bed, then licked up and down on her kitty while she held the lips open for me.

"Umm, baby. Yes, just like momma taught you. Eat me, baby. I need you so much. Only you, son. Only my little man." She moaned and threw her head back as I trapped her clitoris with my lips and sucked hard on it, just the way I knew she liked me to.

I flicked my tongue back and forth across it, while she spread her thick thighs wider, and humped into my face. The springs on the bed started to squeak, and my slurping got louder. I could feel my dick getting harder and harder as I smelled her.

She pushed my head further into her. "Yes! Yes, baby! Honor your mother! Honor me, baby! Honor me like you supposed too! Unnn! Unn! Bay! Beeee!" She screamed and started shaking hard.

I sucked and nipped at her clit, attacking it with no mercy. The more she shook, the harder I sucked until she was pushing me away from her.

"Unn! Bay! Bee! No! More! Please! No More!" she hollered and tried to scoot backward.

I jumped on the bed and straddled her, holding her down while I pushed her negligee up to her breasts. I could feel her hot pussy on my stomach, scalding me. It was wet and leaking her juices. My dick was harder than it had ever been. I needed to be inside of her body. I needed to fuck my momma, just like she had taught me to. I felt her reaching between our bodies, and then she was lining me up to her pink hole. As soon as my head touched her hotness, I slammed him home, biting into my bottom lip.

"Unnn! Bay-beee-ah! Ummmm, you in me again. My baby in me again!" she screamed, then pulled me down, and started to suck allover my lips while I stroked her hard and as deep as I could.

Her pussy juices bubbled around her opening, before dripping down into her ass crack.

I leaned down and sucked her big, brown nipple into my mouth, sucking as if I were her baby, all the while my hips rose and fell, slamming my dick into her with full force. She moaned in my ear loudly.

"This my pussy, momma. You hear me? This mine. Tell me that this pussy belongs to me. Tell me, right now!" I growled, sat up, and put both her legs on my shoulders, and really got to killing that shit.

"Unn! Unn! Unn! It's. Unn! Unn! It's yours! It's yours, baby! Momma! Momma! Momma! Unn! Unn! Pussy! Belongs! To! Her! Unnn! Baby! Her babbeeee! Uhhh! Baby, I'm cuuummming!" She groaned, closing her eyes and turning her head to the side.

The headboard slammed against the wall, and I sped up the pace, long stroking her like she'd taught me to do, putting my abs into it, trying to please her as best as I could because I knew that she needed me to. That was the reason that she had adopted me in the first place.

Her pussy walls got to vibrating, milking me, and the feeling became so intense that I could feel my whole body locking up, and then the feeling of euphoria came over my brain before I felt it shoot down to my balls. As soon as I felt myself getting ready to cum, I pulled out of her and started stroking my dick super-fast. Sista Jones always wanted me to cum allover her breasts and stomach. She said it was her joy to have her baby cum allover her. I didn't know what she meant by that entirely, but I just chalked it up to her being a freak.

I watched string after string of cum shoot across her mid-section.

She jerked in the bed. "Unn! Baby, yes, cum allover yo' momma. Cum allover me, baby; you know I love it." She rubbed it into her skin, then pulled me by my dick until I was kneeling over her. She sucked me back into her mouth, sucking loudly, before licking up and down my stalk; squeezing it, then slowly pulling her fist to the top of the head, causing a thick glob of white to appear before she licked it off and swallowed. "Umm, my lil' man tastes so good." She moaned, licking her lips.

Afterwards, she made me eat her pussy one more time while she told me how much she loved me and that I belonged to her. That I was her only son, and this was how I honored my mother. I did everything that she said do, but most of the time, my mind was on my sister Purity.

Purity was one year younger than me, and when we were taken away to foster care, they split us up, though we were lucky because different families from our church had chosen to take us in. I was adopted by Pastor Jones and his wife, and my sister was adopted by Deacon Robinson and his wife, Gloria. The preacher and his wife had one daughter named Kylie. She was the same age as me, and we even went to the same school out here in Houston.

13

My sister, on the other hand, had to deal with Deacon Robinson, his wife, and their two sons that were a few years younger than her. It seemed like every time I talked to my sister, there was always bad news. It was either the Deacon was trying to come into her bedroom at night, or his sons were trying to do the most to her. Lately, things had been getting worst, so I was trying to find a way to take my sister away from her misery and pain.

I was set to be eighteen in two months, then I would be on my own. I knew that I had to have my bands all the way up so I could support her and myself. Our parents had overdosed together off of heroin when I was just nine years old, and she was eight. We had the same father, but different mothers. She didn't know where her biological mother was, and our father had never made the effort to find her, or at least that's what he had always said. In his opinion, Purity's mother was a lost cause, and not worth the effort it would take to track her down.

Sista Jones sat on the side of the bed, sliding her negligee over her shoulders. I watched her titties bounce a little bit. Her nipples were still hard. "Shemar, I got that three thousand dollars that you said you needed, and I'm going to give it to you in the morning, even though I don't know what you need it for." She looked over her shoulder at me and smiled. "And you still ain't gon' tell me either, are you?"

I sat up and scooted across the bed until I was sitting beside her. I wrapped my arm around her body, laying my hand on her thick thigh. I could smell her well-fucked pussy. It caused me to get hard again, but I tried to ignore it. "Momma, you already know I ain't gon' lie to you, so it's best that we not even get into all of that. What I will say is that I gotta start getting my money up so I can take care of my sister when I turn eighteen. We can't be dependents all of our lives."

She faced me, leaned her head down and bit my chest, before sucking on it, and running her hand across my abs. "But, baby, you know that momma will take care of you. I'll give you whatever you want. You are most important in my life, and you know that." She licked my nipple and opened her thighs wide, exposing her kitty again.

I started rubbing it, playing with her sex lips, while she moaned into my neck. "I gotta get on my grind. I know you'll reach for me, but I gotta get out here hard because I'm finna be a man and I can't depend on you for everything. You can't coddle me forever." I slid two fingers deep into her, feeling her heat. Then, I pulled them out and sucked my fingers, before sliding them back into her. There was nothing like the taste of pussy. She had trained me well.

"Baby, well, you do what you gotta do, but just know that whenever you need me, I'll be there for you, because you are my little man, no matter how big you get. You belong to me, and I will literally die without you." She smiled and ran her thumb across my cheek. "You're so fine. I just pray that no woman ever steals you away from me, because I will seriously end my life if I can't have my little man. You're the only reason I'm still here." She leaned over and kissed my cheek, just as we heard a car pulling into the driveway.

Chapter 2

My best friend was a female who had more balls then most niggas I knew, and more hoes. Her name was Nikki, and she was about that life. We were in foster care together for two years before the Pastor and his wife adopted me, and the Deacon adopted my sister. Nikki was a goon at heart, and like me, she hated niggas and loved money. Her father was an old gangsta that hustled out of Cloverland for damn near thirty years before he got gunned down right in front of her. She was just six years old at that time, and the hitters had even hit her once in the back, leaving her for dead, though she'd survived.

The next day, after Sista Jones gave me that three bands, I met Nikki at an abandoned duplex on Franklin Street. The house was boarded up with green boards, but I knew she was there. I jogged along the gangway until I got to the back of the house, then beat on the back door three times, waited, then hit it four times. That was our special knock. She knew it couldn't be nobody but me, but she still opened the door with a fat ass Glock .40 in her hand. As she opened the door, she had it pointed directly at whoever would be standing outside. In this case, it was me.

She stood there, holding the gun with her eyes lowered into slits, and her long dreads falling across her shoulders. As soon as she saw that it was me, she smiled, but kept the gun aimed at me.

"Whut it dew? Thought yo' ass wasn't gon' be out of bed 'til a lil' later."

I looked both ways, then exhaled, pushing the gun out of my face. "Get that mafucka out my face. You ready to hit somethin'?" I asked as stepped past her and into the duplex. It felt a lil' chilly since it was only nine in the morning, even though the sun was out, and it was mid-April.

Nikki closed the door and put the Glock into the small of her back. I followed behind her as she went up the stairs and into the house. It was completely empty with the exception of a dirty mattress that was on the floor of the living room. I knew it was where she slept on most nights. Ever since her father had been killed, life had been up and down for her. Whereas me and my sister had been adopted, Nikki had escaped the system, and was on the run from them.

She walked over to the bed and sat down on it. "I wanna hit them niggas that sell weed over there on Marshall. It's two of them, and that shit is Loud. I know they be having they whole stash on them, money and all. We can get like five gees if we hit both they ass. You down for that?" she asked, pulling a half a blunt from under her pillow and putting fire to the end of it.

The blunt was real skinny and I could tell that it didn't have that much weed in it; mostly paper.

I nodded. "Yeah, let's hit they ass. We gotta have that paper, ASAP. But that ain't even gon' scratch the surface. It's Monday today, and by the end of the week, I'm trying to see at least ten bands. I gotta start getting right for my sister. I'll be eighteen soon."

Nikki inhaled a thick cloud of smoke and tried to hand me the blunt, but I shook my head.

17

"I'm good, ma. That shit mostly paper, and I ain't trying to be having heart burn and stuff. Don't even trip. Once we hit these niggas, we'll be able to smoke like we need too." Even though I was saying that to her, I was already thinking about how I was gon' sell mine. I needed to get my stacks up, and I needed to do it as soon as I could.

Ever since my seventeenth birthday, I had been saving almost every penny that I came across. At that moment, I had close to eleven thousand dollars, but it wasn't enough to support two people, and I knew that.

Nikki sucked her teeth and waved me off. "Fuck you, then. I'll smoke my shit on my own. You always acting all bourgee and shit." She reached under the bed and came up with a .38 Special, tossing it to me. "If these niggas get out of line, I'm bussing they ass because I ain't got no time for this bullshit. I'm lettin' you know that right now, so we betta be on the same page, because they ain't finna just give us they shit. I hope you know that." She pulled off of the blunt.

Even though I had been raised by the pastor and his wife, my DNA was rotten. I didn't really give a fuck about bussing a nigga because I hated most males in general. I just didn't vibe with them. I felt like a lion. I couldn't see myself having another male lion in my pride. I would hit licks with them, but in the end, I would always be plotting on them; ready to pounce when the time was right.

I looked over the .38 and popped open the chamber, spinning the cylinder, noting that it only had four bullets in it. "Where the other two at, Nikki?" I asked, giving her a crazy ass look.

She was too busy smoking the blunt, but trying her best to not burn her fingers. She dropped it to the carpet and stepped on it. "I used them yesterday. I caught some bitch ass nigga slipping at the gas station, but instead of him handing me over his shit when I reached into his pocket, that fool elbowed me and took off running. I bussed at him twice, and know for sure that I hit him at least once. I just don't know where. So, that's what you got to use, deal with it."

An hour later, I was knocking on the back door to the Shug and LoLo Loud House with a black ski mask already pulled down over my face. I was thinking that as soon as they opened the door, that I was just gon' force my way in and smack the one that opened the door with my burner before aiming it at whoever else was on the other side of the door, then Nikki would come in right behind me on business. It was something that we had did many times before. I just had to keep in mind on what Nikki said about them not just giving us they product without putting up a fight. I was all for the paper, but I didn't really wanna kill these niggas over the lil' chump change that they were sure to have.

I waited another thirty seconds before I beat on the door again, and then a voice came from the other side of the door, asking me what was good?

Nikki situated her mask on her face, and pulled her Glock from the small of her back, cocking it. "Tell them you trying to get right, and they gon' open the door," she whispered, standing on her tippy toes to talk into my ear.

I nodded as the wind blew. "I'm tryna get right, homie. I need a few cuties," I said, slipping the .38 Special off of my waist and crouching down a lil' bit on the side of the backdoor.

There was a brief pause, and then to my surprise, I could hear the lock turning on the door. Then, slowly, the door opened up inch by inch. I could feel my heart beating fast, then it was like the world closed in around me. I got geeked up. with one fast motion, I slammed my shoulder against the door, and pushed it in with all of my might.

It swung inward, and I flew into the house on business with Nikki right behind me. As soon as I saw Shug trying to recover after having the door pushed into him, I smacked him with all of my might with the side of the .38. *Bam!*

He flew into the brick wall along the back steps, holding his face. "What the fuck, man! LoLo, it's a hit, nigga!" he hollered, before dropping to the ground and trying to reach for his pistol.

I kicked him in the chest, and smacked him with the banger again, while Nikki ran up the stairs and into the house. I could hear her shoes squeaking against the linoleum floor.

"Bitch ass nigga, don't move or I'ma pop yo' ass. Test me if you want to!" she hollered. I heard what sounded like a smack, and then *boom!*

"Ahhh! Bitch! What you do that foe!" LoLo hollered.

"Told you I ain't playin' with yo' ass! Now, lay on yo' stomach!"

I smiled under my mask and snatched Shug up by his neck, while blood ran out of the wound on his forehead, and from the split on the left side of his mouth. I put the pistol to his cheek, and got as close to him as possible, looking him straight in the eye. "Check dis shit out, homeboy. All I want is the weed and the paper. I know you niggas holding. Let me clean dis bitch out, and you can leave from this lick with yo' life intact. You play games andI'ma smoke you, my nigga. Dis yo' last warning."

Shug shook his head from right to left. "I'll give you all dis shit, homie, but it don't belong to me. You fuckin' with that nigga Taurus shit, and the homie don't play about his chips." Blood slowly dripped out of his nose, and slid across his lips.

I pressed the pistol so hard into his forehead that it broke the skin. "Homeboy, I ain't ask you all that. Fuck that nigga Taurus, man. I want that paper. Now, lead me to it, or eat these bullets. It's yo' choice." I cocked the hammer and lowered my eyes.

He swallowed, then nodded. "Aiight, potna. Come on, man."

I grabbed him by the back of the neck as he led me upstairs and into the first-floor landing. The crib had a strong aroma of weed, like all they did all day long was smoke, and bag that shit up. It had a few pieces of furniture in it, with a big flat screen television that had an X-Box connected to it. On the screen was the game *Call of Duty* paused. I took that to mean that they were in there playing it when we knocked on the door, ready to hit they ass.

Nikki was in the living room with her foot standing on LoLo's neck while he bled out of his shoulder, laying on his back. He was taking bundles of cash out of his pocket and setting it beside him.

"All yo' pockets, nigga. Turn them bitches inside out. This shit ain't no game," she growled through clenched teeth.

I put my chest to Shug's back and wrapped my arm around his neck. "Take me to the safe, nigga. I know y'all got one in here, so don't play with me," I said, taking a stab in the dark.

You see, I didn't know if they had a safe in there or not, but I just figured that they did, because most of the niggas that hustled out of Trap Houses in Houston had them. I didn't understand why niggas didn't keep safes at their crib where they laid their heads. But then again, it wasn't for me to figure that shit out.

"Give that nigga all that shit, Shug, before this bitch kill me. Fuck that shit! It ain't worth dying for. It's in the back room, in the box spring. Fifteen thousand, and five pounds of Loud. Y'all take that shit and just go, man. Please, don't kill us over this shit. It ain't even ours." LoLo whined, sounding like a straight bitch.

I tightened my grip on Shug's neck, and put the .38 under his chin. "You betta listen to ya' homeboy or I'm splashing you. Then, I'ma make him take me to the stash."

"Ack! Ack! You choking me," he gasped.

I unloosened my grip just a little bit. "Let's go, nigga!"

"Aiight, man, I'll take you to it. Just, please, don't fuck me up no moe." he whimpered, before I pushed him in the back for him to get further down the hallway.

He stumbled, before catching his balance. I wanted to get this weed and money, and get the fuck up out of there. I didn't know who this Taurus nigga was that he called himself warning me about, but I figured that he was one of them major niggas that hustled in Houston. I didn't know how often he checked in on them, but I figured that he had to know that they were bitches, and he didn't allow for them to keep a large portion of his money at a time. Fifteen gees was a lot of money for a weed spot to carry at one time, so I guessed that it wouldn't be long before he was picking up his scratch.

Less than two minutes later, I had Shug to flip over the mattress and dig his hand into the box spring, taking out a bundle of cash again and again until there was a pile at my feet. Then, he started to pull out the pounds of Loud.

"Nigga, wrap all that shit in that sheet right there, and hurry up before I pop yo' ass."

He got to moving so quickly that his blood was being slung all over the carpet. It fell from the crack in his forehead and from his nose. I could hear him swallow a few times. It sounded like he was nearly choking on it.

After all of the money and weed was wrapped securely in the sheet, I slammed the handle of the pistol into the back of his head, causing him to fall forward, with his cheek against the carpet, knocked out cold. I grabbed the sheet and made my way out of the room. When I got into the living room, Nikki had her pistol to LoLo's head with, the hammer cocked back. "Come on. I got everything. We up out dis bitch."

She straddled his chest and shook her head. "Nah, man. Homeboy know who I am. Dis nigga just asked me why I'm doing them like dis when he just gave me a nickel bag of Loud for foe dollaz yesterday. That tell me that he know who I am. I can't have dis shit come back to fuck us over." She wrapped her hand around his neck and put the barrel of her gun into his eye socket.

"I swear I ain't gon' say shit shawty. Dat snitch shit ain't in me, man. I swear I don't get down like dat," he whimpered.

I felt like we had been in there ten minutes too long. If she was gon' kill the nigga then that meant that I had to go and finish off Shug, too. It was apart of the game. I wasn't finna let my homie get into shit that I wasn't gon' back up. "Den smoke dat nigga, shawty. Fuck 'em. I'ma go body dis nigga in here so we can bounce."

"But I—" *Boom!*

I watched the gun jump in her hand before the bullet left the it and slammed into LoLo's eye, punching his brain out the back of his head. It splattered against the carpet.

Nikki stood up and looked down on him, shaking her head. "Damn, I ain't wanna body these niggas over this lil' petty ass money. Fuck!"

I handed her the sheet with all the shit wrapped up in it. "Look, just meet me at yo' crib. I'll be there in a minute."

I made my way down the hallway until I was standing over Shug, who was still knocked out cold, laying on his side. That fool was snoring and everything. Before I could even stop to think about

24

what I was finna do, I knelt and put the .38 to his temple and pulled the trigger. *Boom!* His face jumped from the floor as noodles were punched out the other side of his head.

A few moments later, I was running full speed out of the house, on my way to Nikki's spot, where we split up the cash, and pounds of weed. We wound up walking away with $7,500, and two and a half pounds of weed apiece. I put five gees in my stash, and kept two on me for spending money. The other five was to go to Purity.

Chapter 3

The next morning, I caught Purity coming out of the Deacon's house, on her way to the bus stop. I hadn't seen her in about two days, because I had been so preoccupied with Nikki, trying to figure out things, financial, so I could be in a better position to custody of her after my birthday. I just wanted to make sure that she would need for absolutely nothing when the time came for her to be under my care.

When she came out of the Deacon's house and saw me waiting at the bottom of the stairs, she nearly broke her neck to get down them and into my arms. "Shemar! Oh my God!" She screamed before wrapping her arms around my neck, burying her face into my chest.

I held her for a few moments with my eyes closed, just loving the fact that my sister was crazy about me, and also that she was safe and sound. Every single day that she was Not in my arms, I worried about her safety and well-being. She was my heart. "I missed you so much, Purity. I really have," I said, rubbing her back.

She took a step back and I noted that she had tears running down her cheeks. "I'm ready to go away from here, Shemar. I can't take it anymore. I am tired of this family. They are always trying to do way too much to me. Last night, the Deacon made me give him a massage on his hairy back and I hated it. I hate touching that gross man. I just want to be away from here so bad." She whined, shaking her head, before laying it back on my chest. "I can't wait until you're eighteen."

Every time Purity told me what she had to go through while living at that house, it made me want to kill everybody that lived with her. My little sister meant the world to me, and it made me sick to my stomach to know that I couldn't protect her all of the times that she needed me to. I felt like that was my role in life— to protect her and to make sure that she was always well taken care of. She mattered more to me than I did to myself.

I held her more firmly. "I'm gon' make sure that when it is time for me to take custody of you, that we have absolutely everything that we need. You are my princess, and you deserve nothing less than the best. So, I gotta go hard for us, all the way until it's time for me to take you to our new home. Do you understand me?" I asked, looking into her beautiful face.

She slowly nodded, looking up at me. "I do, and I know that you got us. It's why I fight through what I have to. I just can't wait until it's just me and you. We've been separated by this system for so long, it feels like it's been forever."

I kissed her forehead and pulled her into my embrace, just as the front door to the Deacon's house opened and he appeared with his big belly and suspenders. "Purity, you gone and get to school before you be late. Now, you can talk to him at another time, but not now." He straightened his glasses on his face.

I mugged him with serious hatred, and in that moment, I felt like taking my pistol off of my hip and shooting his bitch ass in the chest while my sister watched. I knew that one day I was gon' torture his ass in front of her for all of the shit that he'd made her do, but I was forced to bide my time.

"Say, Mr. Robinson, I ain't just a him. I'm her brother, so you can address me as such. I shouldn't have to keep on telling you this," I said, feeling myself getting heated.

Purity must have felt my heart beating fast, because she got that worried look on her face. "Calm down, Shemar, it's okay. I'll just meet you around the corner and you can drive me to school. How does that sound?" she whispered, holding my face in both of her hands.

"Purity, I'm not gon' tell you again, young lady. Now, do like I say, or else," the Deacon warned, and I damn near lost my mind.

I moved Purity out of the way and made my way up the stairs in a hurry. "Or else what, Deacon? Huh? What you think you gon' do to my sister later? I'm tired of this shit."

"Shemar, please. No. Please, leave him alone and let's go!" Purity yelled, running up the stairs behind me.

The Deacon wasn't as crazy as I thought, because he ran back into the house and slammed the door. I was so glad that he did, because had he not, I was sure that I would have fucked him up royally over threatening my sister, especially in front of me.

Purity pulled my arm. "Just go, Shemar, and I'll meet you around the corner. We can't have you beefing with him or kicking his ass, because that will make it hard for you to take custody of me when it's time. Think, big bro. You have to be smart, or we're going to be in serious trouble."

I took a deep breath and noted that my chest was heaving. I was steaming mad. I hated the fact that the Deacon had authority over my sister, and that she was basically his property for the time being. I felt like such a loser. I felt powerless. I slowly nodded. "Yeah, you right, Purity. I gotta stay in my game for us. You just meet me around the corner in five minutes, because I need to talk you anyway." I pulled her to me and gave her a firm hug.

She nodded, then I watched as she disappeared into the house, and closed the door.

I jogged to the Preacher's house and jumped in my 1987 Chevy Caprice Classic. It was midnight blue with a few rusted spots on the driver's side door, but the inside was clean. Soon as I got to my whip, I jumped inside of it and pulled away from the curb, just as the Pastor was coming out of the house. Looking in my rear-view mirror, I saw him trying to wave me down, but I ignored him because I wanted to hurry and get to my sister, so I could take her to school.

By the time I pulled around the corner, she was waiting on me with a sad look on her face. I pulled alongside her, leaned over and opened the door, waiting for her to get in. After she sat down and closed the door, she leaned forward and placed both of her hands over her face, before crying her little heart out. I felt sick to my stomach almost immediately. A huge lump formed in my throat and I tried my best to swallow it while I wrapped my right arm around my little sister, and pulled her closer to me.

"What's the matter, Purity? Why are you crying?" I asked as a

school bus rolled down the street that we were parked on. It had stopped and picked up a few kids.

She continued to cry, then removed her hands and shook her head slowly. "I'm just so tired of all of this, Shemar. I wish we didn't have to go through this anymore. I wish they would let you adopt me already. Life just isn't fair. I need you more and more every single day. When I'm in that house, I am all alone and there is no one there to protect me from those monsters. You're all that I have, and I can't even have you when I need you the most." She lowered her head, then the sobbing commenced.

Now, I really felt sick. I felt like throwing up everywhere because of how life was effecting Purity. I felt less than a man because I knew that it was my job to protect my little sister. Because of our current situations, I was not able to. That killed my soul. I felt lower than scum, and was trying to dig deep down within myself to try and find the words that would give her the strength to endure what she was going through until I would be able to pull her out of it. The more I heard her crying, the more my heart split down the middle.

After five minutes of searching within myself to find the right words and came up with nothing, I simply grabbed her closer to me and wrapped both of my arms around her while she laid her head on my chest. "Purity, I just need for you to fight just a little while longer. You know that I won't fail you. As son as I am able to take you away from the Deacon and his family, I am. But when I get you, Purity, I want to make sure that you need for absolutely Nothing at all, because you are my princess, and you deserve the best of the best."

She shook her head and it caused her natural curls to bounce around. "But I don't care about things, Shemar. All I care about is being safe with you. Being in your arms and away from this cold world. We've been going through hell ever since our parents died, and it's not fair. I hate that we can't have normal lives like other kids. You're all that I have, and I need you every day, more and more." She kissed me on the cheek and laid her head back on to my chest.

I rubbed her back, and took a deep breath before exhaling slowly. I felt so sick, because just as much as she needed me, I needed her. I knew what I had to do, and even if it would cost me my last breath, I was going to do it.

I leaned down and kissed her on the forehead, then pulled her away from my chest. I into my pocket and I pulled out five one hundred dollar bills, handing them to her. "Look, I want you to put this in yo' emergency funds. That way, if anything ever takes place and you need to buss a move, or you see somethin' that you want, you can get it right away. I don't want you being dependent on nobody. You are my heart." I rubbed her soft cheek.

She scrunched her face. "But I already got more than three thousand dollars put up. I don't need all of this money, Shemar. You have to stop thinking that you need to spoil me in this way, because I don't care about money. All I care about is being back with you. I hate these people. Then, every time you hand me a bundle of money like this, I always wonder how you were able to get it. Every night, I have nightmares about something happening to you before we can get away from all of this stuff that we're going through, separately." She lowered her head, and shook it. "I can't make it in this world without you. I'm not strong enough, and I swear I just can't. So, please, don't make me." Tears leaked out of her eyes, and her head fell back to my chest.

I hated when Purity cried. It always made me feel so weak. I felt like I'd rather face and fight a hundred niggas at one time than to sit back and watch my little sister cry. I held her more firmly for about ten minutes without saying a single word, and then I remembered that I had to get her to school on time, or the Truancy Officer would be contacting the Deacon, and that would spell trouble for my little sister.

I started up my car and pulled away from the curb. "Purity, keep on stacking the money up when I give it to you. This is the way that it's supposed to be. It's my job to make sure that you are straight at all times. I don't care about us being with these foster families. You are still my responsibility, and I have to make sure that you have everything that you need. It's time for you to get your hair and nails done again too, so use some of that money for that."

She smiled weakly. "You will never listen to me, will you?" she asked, running her fingers through her hair. She looked defeated and a little exhausted. She took the five hundred dollars and put them in her Fendi purse.

"I hear everything that you're saying, and I'm gon' take heed to it. I gotta make sure that you straight. You're my baby sister."

When I got back to the Pastor's house, Mrs. Jones was waiting for me in the living room. As soon as I came through the door, she walked up to me and kissed me on the lips; sucking on them hard, and moaning into my mouth. "I missed you, baby. I been thinking about you all day long." She wrapped her arms around the top of my neck, and kissed my lips again; licking before sucking them into her mouth.

I wrapped my arms around her small waist, then reached down and gripped that fat ass that she was carrying. She had on this red skirt that cuffed her ass. As I rubbed all over her booty, I slowly moved the skirt upward until I was able to slide my hand under it feeling her satin panties. I put my fingers into the leg bands and felt on her hot skin, before easing them into her crease, where I played with her thick, trimmed sex lips.

"Umm, there you go already. Every time I just try and hug you, you always gotta play between my legs. You be driving me crazy." She slid her thighs further apart, giving me access to her box as I rubbed it from the back.

I sucked on her neck, then bit it aggressively. My dick got harder and harder. That woman had a spell on me that I couldn't deny. Every time her scent went up my nose, I turned into an animal. I picked her up into the air, and she wrapped her legs around me.

"Umm, baby. What you finna do to me?" she moaned with her head tilted backward.

I crashed into the wall with her and reached under her to pull her panties to the side so I could get into her pussy. Simultaneously, I wiggled my pants and boxers down my thighs until my dick was standing up and poking the underside of her thigh.

She reached between us and guided me into her hot kitten. I slammed her down on him, before picking her back up, and slamming her back down onto him again. Her box was super wet and tight. I needed to see her titties. I loved how they looked, and how big the nipples were on them. Seeing them always made me go crazy.

"Pull yo' titties out, momma. Please. Let me see 'em." I huffed as I slid her up and down my dick super-fast.

Her back slid against the wall. "Un! Un! Un! Okay, baby! Un! Un! Anything for my baby!" She groaned with her eyes closed.

I watched her take her shoulder straps and pull them off until she exposed her black lace bra. Then, she unhooked it in the front, and both of her brown titties fell out with erect nipples. Just seeing them sent me into savage mode.

I smashed her further into the wall, leaned my head down and sucked on one nipple, and then the next. Biting them slightly, and pulling with my thick lips, I made loud nasty, noises that drove her crazy.

"Unnn! Son! Ummm, baby! I love you so damn much! It feels so good! Now screw me, baby! Screw me as hard as you can. Please," she screamed, and wrapped her arms around my neck super tight.

I leaned back slightly, spread my feet, then got to slamming her down on my dick with no mercy. I plunged into her box at full speed, while she screamed and moaned in my ear. That pussy was so good that I felt like crying. The way it gripped me, how slippery she was, and the noises in my ear was enough to whip me one hundred percent, if I wasn't used to that level of fuckin, but I was. Like I said before, she'd been going in on me ever since I was a young teen, so I was well trained. I never held the things that we did against her. I was actually thankful for them, as crazy as that sounds. I think that most young dudes wished that they had an older female to show them the ropes, and if she was one that was already in the house with you, then that just made it that much better. It was that behind closed doors kind of love that made it that much better.

I fell to the carpet with her and really got to beating here box in with all of my might, while she squeezed her eyelids together, and tears ran down her cheeks. "I love dis pussy, Mrs. Jones. I swear I love it." As soon as I felt her shaking under me, it brought on my own climax.

I sped up the pace, clenched my teeth together, and then I was cumming in her while my abs tightened.

After we were finished, we showered together. As I was sliding my boxers up my thighs, she was fixing her hair in the mirror. I was off from school that whole week. All seniors in Houston were, for exams week. The Pastor worked in the mornings at a Real Estate company, and their daughter was only a junior, so she was at school. I already knew that me and the Pastor's wife would be getting it in the whole week I was off.

Mrs. Jones looked at me through the mirror. "You know the Deacon called me this morning, saying that you were trying to beat his butt over your sister. Now, you know you can't be doing that, Shemar. Are you trying to get arrested or something? Do you have any idea what they'll do to your pretty self in prison, with those green eyes and that natural wavy hair? Huh?"

I scrunched my face as I slid into my pants. I was thinking that if she knew how I got down that she definitely wouldn't be asking me no questions like that. "I don't know what they do in prison, Mrs. Jones, but whatever they do, they wouldn't be doing it to me." I put my black beater on and tucked it into my pants. "Besides, that Deacon ain't gotta be talking to my lil' sister the way that he do, especially in front of me. I didn't get on no bull with him until he came at her bogus. I can't wait until I'm eighteen."

Mrs. Jones turned around and faced me with her bottom lip poked out. "You gon' leave your momma, then? Huh? Are you gon' leave me here, all alone with that boring man?" She stepped forward and kissed my lips before dropping to her knees and kissing the crotch of my Polo Black Labels.

I looked down on her, then pulled her up and hugged her. I could feel her naked titties against my chest. "I'll never leave you ma. But I gotta make it happen for my sister. I gotta take custody of her before the Deacon and his family hurt her in a way that will destroy her forever. It's my job to protect her, by any and every means."

She reached her hand under my shirt and rubbed my stomach muscles. "I know it is, baby, and I'm willing to help you in any way that I can, just as long as you never leave me for good. I need access to you, always. You have me hooked."

I didn't know what to say to that, but I knew I had to figure out a way in which she could be beneficial to me and my sister. I honestly loved Mrs. Jones, and if I could prevent it, I would never allow for anything to happen to her. But my sister was my world, and I would do anything for her, and use anybody, as long as it would benefit Purity.

Chapter 4

Later, that same day, I met up with Nikki at one of her girlfriends' cribs on Park Place. I sat on the couch and bagged up four ounces of Loud in all dimes, because it wasn't nobody around the hood doing that. Everybody that sold weed was selling it at a minimum of twenty dollars a bag. Since I wanted to jump into the game and get my weight up, I decided that I would sell my bags for half the price as everybody else, yet make my bags nearly the same size as theirs. I wasn't really one of them hustling type of niggas, though. I loved fast money, and the fastest way to money for me was taking that shit by the gun, so I was finna have Nikki's girlfriend's brother, Tim, push my product.

Nikki sat down on the couch across from me, then Tameka came and sat on her lap. Tameka was a short red bone that was crazy strapped with big titties. She was dark skinned, with some fake hazel eyes. She had a two-year-old son, but she was Nikki's bae. I didn't know if she still fucked with niggas or, but she did have a kid.

I dropped the last bag into my Ziploc and ended my total at five thousand dollars. "When Tim supposed to get here? I thought you said he was on his way," I said, looking at Tameka as Nikki sucked on her neck and slid her hand into her biker shorts.

I watched her spread her thighs, then Nikki's hand started to move up and down. Tameka moaned, licked her lips, and closed her eyes. "Umm. He just hit my phone ten minutes ago, saying he was on his way. So, he should be here in a minute." She licked her lips again, then bit into her bottom one. "Nikki, why don't you come back here into my room real quick, so we can handle this business. I need some of you. You know it ain't gon' take me that long to get right," she whimpered.

Nikki smiled, and bit her on the neck. "N'all. Me and Shemar gotta go handle some business, but I'll come fuck with you tonight, after we done."

I noted her hand moved faster and faster between Tameka's thighs. Tameka squeezed her eyelids tighter and opened her legs further. She placed her feet onto the arm of the couch. "Unnn! Shit, Nikki! Fuck, Nikki! Get that shit, Nikki! Get it! Finger this pussy! Finger meeee! Oh, shiiitttt! I'm cuming, bitch!"

Nikki bit her neck, and got to fingering her so fast that sweat appeared on her forehead. Once Tameka started shaking, she fingered her for a while longer, then pulled her fingers out of her biker shorts and sucked them into her mouth loudly, slobbering all over them. "Dis my bitch, right here. Pussy taste good as a muthafucka."

Tameka dropped down in front of her and started to unbutton Nikki's Gucci pants, but Nikki pushed her away. "Please, Nikki, let me eat that shit while Shemar watch. You always saying that shit turn you on even more when he in the room, watching us," she said, breathing hard. She looked over at me while sucking on her bottom lip. I could see that her nipples were poking through her tight white blouse.

At hearing that, my dick started to rise, because even though Nikki fucked with nothing but females, she was still bad as hell, and real thick. She was feminine, with the heart of a savage. We never did anything together in a sexual manner, but trust and believe it had crossed my mind on more than one occasion. I just never wanted to cross those lines with her, because I felt that it would jeopardize our relationship. To me, what we had was priceless, though if ever given the green light by her, I would go, ASAP.

Nikki pushed Tameka away, just as Tim came into the crib along with one of his homies by the name of Q.

A few minutes later, I was sitting Tim down and explaining to him how I wanted shit to go with my product. "Look, lil' homie, this is five gees worth of Loud. Forty-five hundred of it is mine, and the other five hundred is yours. Just keep in mind that you don't see a penny until I see all of mine; you understand that?"

He nodded. Tim was two years younger than me. Real fat, but smart to the streets. He knew how to maneuver around Cloverland, and I had a lil' faith in him. I had known him ever since he was about ten years old. "That's cool, man. I can handle this lil' shit, but I am gon' need some to smoke. So, how that work?"

I smiled. "Nigga, now you know that you can't be trying to smoke this shit and sell it at the same time. That won't work. I'm letting you know now that I ain't gon' play about my paper. I don't give a fuck how petty it is." I was serious too. I wouldn't hesitate to pop his ass if he fucked up in even the slightest, because I felt like every penny that I hustled up was meant for Purity's stability.

40

He waved me off. "Nigga, I already know, and you ain't supposed too. I got this shit. I just wanna know if I can get some for myself."

I shook my head. "Hell n'all. That's for making money only. You wanna buy some of that shit, you do that and add that paper to that forty-five hundred I got coming, otherwise it's gon' be a problem."

I got the feeling right then that I shouldn't even fuck with dawg, because I felt like I was gon' have to buss his brain somewhere down the line, and that was only setting myself up for failure. Had I had anybody else that could have pushed that Loud for me, I would have, but I couldn't think of anybody that I trusted more than him, and I didn't have it in me to sit around and get slow money like that. I needed mine in bulk, and I needed it fast.

Nikki took about a half an ounce and tossed it to him. "There you go, Tim. You and yo' lil' nigga smoke on that while y'all pop that shit for my homie right here. Time is money, and don't fuck up, or else shit look real dim for you; trust me. I'ma put something together for you too, Q, once y'all handle that shit for him. First, you gotta show and prove yo' worth, nah mean. My temper way worse than his."

Tameka straddled her, leaned down and sucked on her neck. "That's because you need me to release some of that pent-up frustration that's going on inside of you. Come on, baby, please."

Nikki shook her head, and looked over Tameka's shoulder. "Y'all heard me, right?"

They nodded in unison.

An hour later, we were back at Nikki's Trap, sitting on the dirty ass mattress while I loaded up the

.38 Special with latex gloves on. "How much you think these niggas finna be holding?" I asked, watching her roll a fat ass blunt of the Loud we'd hit Shug and LoLo for.

She licked it one last time, then set fire to the end of it. "We should get ten gees apiece. This lil' bitch that's on my line, setting up her baby daddy because that nigga trifling as hell. She say he got stupid paper, but he don't do shit for they daughter. She texted me about twenty minutes ago and said she already at his stash house, and they sipping on Lean, then they gon' fuck. I guess the nigga get real reckless when he on that drank." She took a strong pull, then blew the smoke out of her nose.

I replaced the cylinder on the gun, and put it into the small of my back. The Trap was dark, with the exception of three big candle burning in the center of the room. I had already seen more than one rat run across the floor, with their red eyes searching, I imagined, for food. "All that sound cool, but how do you know the lick gon' be for twenty gees?" I asked as she passed me the blunt. I took two quick pulls and inhaled deeply.

She shook her head. "I don't know that for sure, but she saying that it should be at least twenty racks in his safe. But you know how this shit go. We ain't gon' know until we actually in that muhfucka." She took her Glock and pulled out the clip, popping the bullets on the bed, counting them one at a time.

I passed her back the blunt as I felt the effects of the Loud taking over me, almost immediately. My eyes got heavy, and the room seemed to get a little stuffy. I also felt paranoid. For what? I don't know.

"Look, you already know how I get down. I mean a lick is a lick, but if we get over here and it ain't that much cash in this safe, then shawty gotta pay, one way or the other." I didn't know how far I would go, but I was gon' be heated if shit didn't turn out the way I wanted it too in my head. I would have settled for another quick five gees, so as long as I got at least that, I would be cool. "Speaking of that safe, do she got the combination?"

Nikki shook her head. "N'all, but that fuck nigga do. As long as he know it, we gon' know it too before its all said and done." She laughed at that, and took another strong pull from the blunt.

I was down for whatever. My high was feeling good, and I was ready to make a nigga cough up them chips by any means.

We finished smoking that blunt, then smoked one more before we got up and headed to the nigga's trap we was getting ready to hit. The chick that was setting up her baby daddy was named Chelsey. I really didn't know her like that, but a few times I'd seen her with Nikki on some late-night creeping shit. Then again, I saw most niggas' baby mother's in Cloverland creepin' with Nikki at one time or another. Nikki always said that every female in the world had a little bi-sexual in her, and that given the right opportunity, that they would get down with a female. After seeing her body count, I believed her.

We waited until about three in the morning before Nikki texted Chelsey. I don't know what she said to her exactly, but what I do know was that when we got to the apartment, the side patio door was unlocked, because Nikki walked right up to it and pulled it open a lil' bit. I situated my black ski mask on my face and took the .38 Special out of the small of my back. Then, I looked alongside of the house, to the front, where I saw that this nigga had a candy coated, purple Lexus, sitting on twenty-eight inch, gold rims, parked in front of the house.

I got to hearing all kinds of caching noises in my head. I felt if that nigga was pushing something like that, then he had to have chips stashed somewhere.

Nikki crouched down and pulled out her Glock, before sliding the patio door open enough for her to slip inside, with me right behind her. My heart was pounding in my chest, and my high seemed like it increased. I never really liked to be under the influence when I hit licks, because I wanted to be on point, but I had let my guard down and got to smoking with Nikki's ass. Right then, I was wishing that I hadn't.

As soon as I stepped foot into the apartment, I smelt pussy and the strong odor of sex. It smelt like they had been fucking for a few hours, and prior to that the muhfuckas hadn't washed their ass or something. Blaring out the speakers was the sounds of SZA, and off into the distance was the distinct sounds of moaning and groaning, along with bed springs going haywire. I smiled under my mask because I knew that this nigga was all the way off of his square. That would make things a whole lot easier.

Nikki held her Glock over her head and cocked it. I pulled back the hammer on mine, ready to buss anything or anybody that jumped out at me. Straight from the patio, we entered into the living room. There was a big 4K television hanging on the wall with the Houston Rockets game playing on it. The living room was decked out with a three-piece white leather furniture set, and glass tables. We ducked alongside of the couch and made our way to the bedroom, following the sex noises. The only thing on my mind was that I was hoping we didn't have to kill this nigga or Chelsey. I mean, if we had to, we had too, but I just wanted shit to go smoothly. The police was still combing the hood real tough over Shug and LoLo's murders. I could only imagine how shit would get if we bodied two more people, only eight blocks over.

When we got outside the door, Nikki held up one finger, then put her small hand over the door knob, and started to turn it slowly until it clicked. Once that happened, she pushed the door in, and the fucking noises was really loud. I ain't even gone lie, it sounded like homeboy was tearing Chelsey's ass up, and the sounds were getting to me in a way I didn't want them to. I felt my shit getting hard, and that was weird, to say the least.

Nikki pushed the door open enough for us to crawl through on our stomachs. The air tasted like sex. It smelled strong as hell, and that made my head cloudy. I got all the way to the side of the bed as it rocked back and forth with the headboard slamming into the wall. The room was illuminated by one candle, and the digital face from their stereo player.

"Take this dick, bitch! Take this dick! I told you I was gon' beat this pussy in! Didn't I! Didn't I!" The nigga growled and the slamming of the headboard got louder and faster.

"Yes, daddy! Yes! Ohhh! Shit, yes! Fuck me! Please, keep on fucking me just like that!" Chelsey hollered.

I jumped up on the side of them and noted that he had her knees pushed to her chest, fucking her like a mad man. I couldn't really make out her face because he was a big nigga, and he was all over her. Grabbing him by the dreads, I smacked him across the face with my pistol, while Chelsey screamed. Only, Chelsey wasn't in the bed with him. It was a Mexican chick who looked terrified.

"Get yo' punk ass out the pussy and take me to the safe, my nigga, or I'm wetting you," I said as he fell backward, holding his face.

"Bryan, who are these people?" the Mexican chick hollered before Nikki smacked her so hard with her pistol that she flew off of the bed, and landed on the floor face first.

Nikki got on to her back and pulled her up by her long hair, causing her to scream again. "Bitch, all we want is the money. Tell that nigga to get that shit or I'm killing you myself." She yanked her head back more forcefully.

I grabbed a handful of Bryan's dreads and stuck my .38 into his cheek. "How 'bout that safe, homie? Let's hurry up." Blood ran out of his nose into his mouth.

I could hear him swallowing it loudly. "I don't know what you talking about. I ain't got no safe in here, man. All I got is a few hundred in my jeans over there, and you can have that shit. Gone 'head."

I definitely was gon' take them hundreds he was talking about, but I wasn't finna settle for just that shit. I knelt and punched him right in his mouth, hard. I mean, I tried to knock a few teeth out of his mouth. His head jerked backward, and he laid flat out on his side, knocked out cold. I smacked the shit out of him, jarring his ass awake.

He woke up, panicking. "Uh! Uh! Why the fuck you doing this, man? You can have that lil' chump change, but I ain't got no safe. I swear."

Nikki slammed the Mexican chick's face into the wooden floor, knocking her out cold. Then, she got up and walked over to where I had him held down. She aimed her gun at his shoulder. "Nigga, where the safe? Last time I'm asking you, too."

His eyes got as big as saucers. I could feel him shaking. "Um, um, who told y'all I got a safe in here, man? I swear, I ain't got no safe. If I did, I would have already told you."

She grabbed a pillow off of the bed, pressed it to his shoulder, and bussed her gun. *Boom!* The sound was muffled, but loud enough to let you know that she popped his ass.

Bryan jumped up and hollered. "Aww! Muthafucka, you shot me in my gotdamn shoulder!" He started to shake.

The smell of gunpowder and burnt pillow was heavy in the room. I slammed his face into the floor, and stuck my pistol into his ear, jamming it hard, so much so that it started to bleed. "Where them bands at, my nigga?"

"Awright! Awright! Awright! Come on, man. Take me to the bathroom. It's at the end of the hallway. My safe behind my medicine cabinet. The money in there. Y'all can have that shit. Just don't shoot me no moe, man. I can't take this shit."

I scrunched my face. "N'all, fuck that, bitch nigga. Give me the combo and I'll go open that shit. You gon' stay yo' punk ass right here until I get back." I pressed the gun harder into his ear. "What is it?"

"Aww, shit. It's foe, twenty-seven, eighty-foe. Start with it to the left, and that bitch gone pop open on the last number. I swear, man. Aww, shit, I'm bleeding. Y'all, don't let me die. Please," he whimpered.

Nikki stood over him and put the Glock to his forehead. "Go handle that business, bruh. If this nigga lying, then I'm splashing his ass with no mercy. Hurry up." She sat on his stomach and put the barrel of the gun on his lips. "Open yo' mouth and suck on the Glock's dick until my homie get back."

I shook my head when he actually did it, then I disappeared into the hallway and made my way to the end of it. There were two incents burning along it. They smelled like sandalwood.

When I got to the bathroom door, I pushed it in and searched along the side of the wall for a switch. When I found it, I flipped it on, illuminating the bathroom before going to the mirror and opening it. It was filled with all kinds of prescription drugs that I didn't give no fuck about. I knocked them all into the sink and tried to pull out the shelves that they were sitting on to see if there was some sort of latch that popped it open, but I found none.

I searched along the side until I felt something poke my finger. As soon as it did, I pinched it, then pulled. Low and behold, the back of the mirror made a loud clicking noise, and then it opened up to reveal a digital faced Secure Lock safe. I took a deep breath and slowly blew it out. I punched in the code that Bryan had given us.

Foe, twenty-seven, eighty-foe. The screen on the digital face flashed green seven times, and then it popped open, sounding like air was being let out of a tire.

I got giddy and opened it all the way to reveal ten separate stacks of money, and two silver packs that were taped heavily. I ran out of the bathroom, back into the bedroom that they were in. and grabbed a pillow. Then, I ran back into the bathroom where I loaded up everything into the pillowcase. I even tossed in the pills that I knocked carelessly into the sink earlier. I didn't know if they could be worth something, but I wasn't taking no chances. After I got all that shit, I jogged back into the room where Nikki was. She was straddled over Bryan with the pistol to his head.

"Let's go. I got everything. Fuck that nigga," I said, ready to get up out of there.

She shook her head. "N'all, man. This nigga know who I am. He just said my name before you came back in here. He talkin' 'bout he know Chelsey put me up to dis. I can't let dis nigga live."

I frowned because I knew what that meant, and I was pissed about it. This was the second lick that we'd been on where the mark was able to identify her. I was starting to think that it was hazardous for us to be knocking niggas off that was in her circle of prey, because they were able to point her out so well. I was ready to get the shit over with.

Bryan had blood pouring out of his nose and mouth. Both eyes were swollen. He looked like a melted Halloween mask. "I swear, y'all can have that shit. I ain't gon' say nothing. I'm gon' take it out on my bitch. Y'all just hitting a lick. This ain't got shit to do with y'all. I swear."

Now I knew that this nigga was foul. I wasn't going for that. If he was soft enough to take out all of his frustrations on a female, then I felt like he was one of them type of niggas that would get the police involved. I was thinking about Purity and being taken away from her, just because I allowed for this nigga's life to be spared. Fuck that.

"Body that nigga then, and let's get up out of here."

As soon as Bryan heard me say that, he jerked upward and flipped Nikki off of him, causing her to crash into the dresser.

Ghost

Chapter 5

Bryan shot up and made his way toward the window, ass naked. I guess he felt that he was about to jump out of it, and that he would have a better chance of surviving if he did that, but I had something else on my mind.

Before he could even get to the window, I let his back have it. *Boom! Boom! Boom! Boom!* Big holes filled him with smoke coming out of them. He leaped into the air, and fell face first through the window, causing it to shatter loudly.

By this time, Nikki had recovered, and so did the Mexican chick. She started to scream before Nikki aimed and sent two bullets through her forehead, spraying the wall with her brains.

When we got back to Nikki's trap, I was heated. I paced with my gun still in my hand. That was four bodies in a matter of days. I didn't give a fuck about the lives; I was worried about the police. I kept on imagining them taking me away from my sister, and then her being stranded in this cold world without me. I would never be able to live with myself. Then, on top of that, I knew they loved to fry niggas in Texas.

Nikki grabbed a bundle of cash and sat it to the side on the bed. "Nigga, you need to chill. It turns out that it was more than twenty stacks in there. It was forty-two. We get twenty one apiece." She held the money up to me.

I stopped in my tracks and mugged her lil' ass. Right in that moment, her lil' pretty face wasn't even doing it for me. "You realize we just killed two more mafuckas, and it ain't even been a week yet? Huh?"

She exhaled and rolled her eyes. "And? So, what that mean? You know that's apart of the game, so why the fuck you so stressed out. What? You turning bitch or somethin'?" she asked, sounding irritated.

I wanted to snatch her lil' ass up and choke her out. Every time I got to speaking logic, she got to making it seem like I was turning into a bitch. Had it been anybody else, I would have bussed them in they shit, but she was my second heart behind my sister. I took a deep breath. "What I'm saying is that we making ourselves hot, and shit ain't gotta be like that. Every muhfucka we done hit was able to make out who you were. That means you slipping, or you hitting muhfuckas that're too close. We can't kill everybody we rob. You understand how stupid that shit is?"

She reached for a cigar and got to bussing it down the middle, preparing to roll a blunt. "Nigga, you tripping. Fuck them niggas, and fuck that bitch. Shit happens. I don't feel bad at all. We all gon' die one day, and its already written how. So, it is what it is. That's how I feel." She started to sprinkle large chunks of Loud up and down the cigar, before rolling it up, and sealing it with the spit from her lips.

I grabbed my twenty-one bands and rolled them up into the pillowcase. In my mind, it was a nice lick. I just wished we hadn't had to kill the two that we did. Once again, fuck their lives. I was worried about the law. "Give me that Glock. I'm getting rid of that mafucka, and this .38. Between the two, they got four bodies on 'em. They'll track us by that alone if ever these pistols are found.

Nikki flicked her lighter and lit the tip of the blunt, then inhaled deeply. Reaching into the small of her back, she handed me the Glock. "Do what you do, Shemar. I'm gon' get me another one tomorrow, now that I got some money to play with. Just make sure you break that bitch down first, and soak it in some bleach overnight before you get rid of it."

I waved her ass off because I already knew what to do. I wasn't a rookie to the streets. "Anyway, we gotta chill with hitting niggas in Cloverland for a minute, because once the law gets wind of Bryan and ole girl, they gon' be all over this muhfucka like white on rice. What you gon' do about Chelsey, because you already know she can't live either?"

Nikki yawned and stretched her arms over her head while she kept the big blunt in her mouth. After stretching, she took the blunt and set it in the ashtray. "I'ma handle her in a few hours. I just need to get a little sleep. Don't worry, I got this."

Something told me right then to just hit the streets with her and go over to Chelsey's house to body her ass, but I gave Nikki the benefit of the doubt. I snatched up my kilo of dope, left her with one, and bounced from her crib with a little worry in my heart.

When I got to the Pastor's house, the sun was just starting to come up, and I was exhausted. I was thinking about catching my sister before she went to school, but I was so weak that I didn't think I had the energy to. The Pastor and Mrs. Jones had a daughter by the name of Simone who was so fine that it was often hard for me to keep my eyes and hands off of her. They didn't let her do nothing or go nowhere. She was one of them females that had parents so strict that it was almost a guarantee that when she got on her own, that she would rebel against them. Well, in Simone's case, she didn't wait until she got on her own. Since they didn't ever allow for her to leave the house, all of her pent-up frustrations that were caused by them, she relayed on to me.

This day, when I got home, she must've been waiting up. As soon as I came through the door, she was already standing in front of it with one finger pressed to her lips, telling me to shush. I noted that the house was quiet, and that the Pastor's car was already gone out of the driveway.

I closed the door behind me and sat the pillow case down, looking over her shoulder into the house. "Girl, what you doing woke already? It ain't even five yet."

She stepped forward and kissed me on the cheek. "I want you to give me some of this dick before I go to school. I need it. My pussy been wet all night, thinking about you. I'm hurting down there," she whimpered, biting on her bottom lip.

She had on a real short, white gown that stopped at the top of her thighs. I figured that they had bought it for her when she was little, and had not got around to buying one that actually fit. Simone was built just like her mother. She was thick and real pretty with it. Both of her nipples were already poking through her gown's top, and I could tell that she wasn't wearing a bra.

She reached and gripped my piece through my pants. "Hurry up before my momma wake up."

I felt my dick jerk a few times as I imagined getting inside of her box. Over the years, we had played around a lot, but I had never managed to get my dick all the way into her before she was hollering that it was hurting too much. It usually ended with me eating her kitty until she came, then I would just grind my pipe between her sex lips until I came all over her stomach.

"Simone, you know you ain't finna let me fuck fa real, so why you playin'?" I asked, pulling her to me and rubbing all over her big booty. It was hot and soft. Every time I thought about her being a virgin, it made me want to kill that pussy.

"Ummm. Yes, I am. I been playin' with it, and now I'm ready. I got three fingers in there a few hours ago, and they didn't hurt. Well, it did, but it felt good. Just give me some for five minutes. Please? I'm so horny," she moaned, humping into me.

I squeezed that ass a little harder. Then, I slid my hand under her gown and rubbed her hot skin, trailing my fingers to her crease. She didn't have a lick of hair there, and that shit drove me nuts. Her pussy was dripping wet. I could smell it and everything. I felt her hump into me again, and by this time, my dick was standing straight up along my stomach, past my navel, throbbing. "Aiight, go to yo' room. I'm on my way," I said, out of breath.

Instead of her allowing for me to follow behind her, she grabbed my hand and pulled me along with her until we got into her room, where she closed the door behind us. As soon as the door closed, I picked her lil' ass up and carried her to the bed. I sat her on it, pushing her back, and opening her thick thighs wide.

I still couldn't believe how thick she was. As soon as them thighs opened, I stuck my face between them, and licked up and down her crease, before sucking her sex lips into my mouth and slurping up the juices that was pouring out of her.

"Unnn, Shemar, you gon' drive me crazy. You already know I can't take it when you get to licking on me," she moaned, arching her back with her mouth wide open.

I smashed her lips together and sucked on them, then spread them all the way apart, exposing her pink. I took my tongue and pushed it into her as far as it would go, tasting her saltiness. My dick was as hard as a brick. The wetter she became, the more I got to imagining myself going as deep into her as I could possibly reach. I stabbed my head back and forth, digging into her center while she shook on the bed, grabbed a pillow and put it over her face, moaning into it.

"You taste good, Simone. This pussy ready for me. I can taste it. You think you ready?" I asked before locking my lips around her clitoris, and sucking it like I was trying to milk her. When I did that to her mother, it drove her crazy, so I figured that the apple shouldn't have fallen too far from the tree. I was right.

Simone screamed into the pillow, wrapped her thick thighs around my face, and got to humping into my mouth like her life was dependent on it.

"Huhhhhhh! Ummm-uh!" She groaned, shaking like she was having a seizure of pleasure.

I felt her squirting all over my lips, and it turned me on even more. I got to thinking about how I was playing with the Preacher's daughter's pussy in his house, and that taboo aspect just made it all the better. After she came, she hopped off of the bed and knelt in front of me, trying to unbuckle my pants in a frenzy. I helped her. My dick popped out, already super hard.

She took him into her little hand and stroked him up and down, moaning while she sucked on her bottom lip. "I want this dick so bad, Shemar. I want you to put it in me. I swear I can take it now. I'm not no little girl no more." She kissed the head, then licked it from the bottom of my stalk, all the way to the top of the head. Then, she sucked me into her mouth, slurping loudly while moaning all around him. She popped him up and rubbed him against her cheek. "You gon' put it in me or not?" she whimpered.

I pulled her up and kissed her on the lips. I reached between our bodies and rubbed all over her bald pussy, separating the lips, slipping my middle finger into her. She moaned into my neck. Her hole was tight. I didn't see me being able to get into her without it hurting, and her screaming would definitely wake up her mother. I pinched her clitoris, causing her to yelp.

"Simone, I want this pussy bad, baby, but I ain't finna be able to fit in you, baby. We gon' have to do this at another time. That way, I can do it right." I kissed her neck, then bit it. She shivered. "You hear me, baby?" I slid a finger back into her tight hole, making her stand on her tippy toes with her eyes closed.

She nodded. "Okay, but can you at least give me the head? You ain't gotta go all the way in me. Just give me the head. I'm begging you." She sat on the bed and opened her thighs wide, reaching between her legs and holding her sex lips apart with two fingers. "Just the head, Shemar. You gotta feel inside of me." She licked her thick lips and opened her thighs some more.

I grabbed my dick, stroking him up and down before I got between her legs and slid him into her wet crease. Her pussy juice was oozing out of her and running down to her thick ass cheeks. Her scent was heavy in the air.

"Just the head, right? That's all you can handle right now?" I gasped, feeling my heart pounding in my chest.

"Ummm. Please, Shemar. Give me a taste, baby. I'm begging you to," she whimpered, rubbing her clit in a circular motion.

Just watching her alone was about to make me cum. This was the Pastor's daughter, and her lil' ass was begging for the pipe. That shit was hot to me.

I eased forward and my head sunk into her hotness. Her sex lips seared each side of my helmet. As soon as it got to the point where I was about to enter into her kitty, she started shaking, and screaming at the same time.

"Uh! Uh! Yesssss! Shemarrrrrr!" Her body went into convulsions.

Instead of me getting the chance to enjoy what I was feeling, I was too busy trying to put my hand over her mouth to shut her up, but it was too late. There was already knocking at her door.

I pulled my dick out of her and popped him back into my boxers, pulled my pants up and got ready for Sister Jones to snap the fuck out.

Doom! Doom! Doom! "Simone, open this damn door, right now. I know Shemar in there with you. I'm finna kick both of y'all asses!" she threatened, and that made my stomach turn upside down.

I wasn't worrying about her whooping me. I knew she wasn't gon' do that. I just worried how this was going to affect mine and her relationship. I wished that I had thought about that before I went into her daughter's room.

Simone hurried and pulled her gown down, then jumped out of the bed with her eyes bugged out of her head. She looked like she wanted to jump out of the window. "What do we do?" she asked in a panic.

I held up a hand. "Just chill, I got her. When I step out of the room, you hurry up and close the door behind me. Do you hear me?" I asked, taking a deep breath.

She nodded, and a single tear fell down her cheek. "I pray she don't put you out. I need you Shemar. I swear I do. I can't be in this house without you." She stepped forward and kissed me on the lips, completely catching me off guard.

I gripped that ass, then broke us apart.

Doom! Doom! Doom! Doom! "Y'all better open this door or I swear for living God that I'm calling Vincent!" Mrs. Jones promised.

Ghost

Chapter 6

As soon as I opened the door, Vicki, the Pastor's wife, tried to rush into the room and attack Simone. I picked her up into the air and carried her back into the hallway while she struggled against me.

"Let me go, Shemar! I'm finna kick her little tail! She up in my house, behaving like a harlot. I ain't going!" She wiggled real hard, and I almost dropped her.

"Momma, chill. It ain't her fault. We was just in there playing around. It ain't that serious," I said, carrying her down the hall toward her room.

We got through the doors and I flopped her on the bed, closing the door behind me. I blocked her from getting back out of the room.

She jumped up from the bed and ran at me. "Move out of the way, baby. I gotta go whoop her ass. She knows better than that," she said with her face scrunched.

I honestly didn't think it was fair that she was trying to blame everything on Simone when, clearly, I had a hand in it as well. I felt like she was scared to discipline me or something.

She tried to get out of the door once again, but I blocked her path. "Shemar, move. I'm not gon' tell you again."

I walked up on her until my forehead was against hers. "Momma, you need to chill. We was just in there playing. Now, I need you to forgive us, because it's both of our fault. I need you to, because me and her didn't really go all the way. That's what I need you for. I need this body." I knew that she loved to hear me tell her that I needed her. It always made her so soft for me, and that was how I needed for her to be, because if she told the Pastor about me and Simone, he was sure to kick me out into the streets and beat Simone senseless. I'd heard him whoop her before and it made me want to kill his ass.

Mrs. Jones lowered her head, and then looked up into my eyes. "Why do you need her, Shemar. I thought I was all that you needed in this house. I thought you loved mommy more than everybody else here." Her voice started to break up and it made me feel some type of way.

I wrapped my arms around her, and held her against my chest. "I do love you more than everybody else here. I don't need her. We was just playing around. All I need is you, momma. You already know that." I kissed her perfumed neck and trailed my hands down to her ass, where I squeezed.

She shook her head. "No, that ain't right, though. You can't be screwing my daughter and me too. I'm yo' momma. I'm supposed to be all that you need. You supposed to honor me."

I rubbed all over that big ass, then started to pull the short skirt up she was wearing. "I know momma, and I'm sorry. Can I have some of you right now, though? Can yo' baby have some of this body that drives me crazy?" I bit into her neck, took a step back, and lowered the straps of her blouse. I pulled them down to her stomach, taking the blouse along with them.

She wore a purple Prada bra. I unlatched it in the front, and both of her breasts fell out with engorged nipples. I pushed them together and started to suck on one nipple, and then the next, making loud noises that I knew drove her insane. She fell on the bed with me on top of her, sucking for dear life.

She pulled up her skirt, and I watched her slide her hand into her panties, rubbing frantically. "This ain't right, Shemar. Umm, baby, this ain't right. You can't be going from her bedroom to mine. I'm yo' momma," she whimpered, and humped into her hand that was going crazy inside of her panties.

I bit into her neck and held the skin with my teeth. "Don't lie, momma. That turn you on, don't it?" I sucked her neck, then bit into it again. I ran my finger under her nose. "Smell that pussy, momma. Smell what yo' baby been doing in the other room." I rubbed them on her upper lip.

She humped into her hand again and started to rub way faster than before. "Stop, son. You can't do me like that. I don't want to smell what y'all been doing. Please." Her legs opened wider.

I pulled her panties to her thighs so I could see what she was doing, and it was just like I thought. She had two fingers going in and out of her box at full speed while she humped into them.

I lowered my head until I was between her legs, sucking on her clit while she fingered herself. Every now and then I would raise my head to entice her further. "You love yo' babies playin' around, momma. That shit drives you crazy, and it's yo' fault because you got me this way. You turned me into a freak like you. Now I want some of my momma's pussy." I got between her legs and put her thighs on my shoulders. "Tell me you want yo' baby. Tell me that it drives you crazy that I was in there playin' with her pussy like I was, but that I still need you. Tell me, momma." I put my dick head right on her wet opening.

She reached between and tried to force me to put it inside of her, but I held my ground.

I needed to hear her tell me what I already knew. "Tell me, momma!"

She whimpered, closed her eyes, and bit into her bottom lip. "Please, don't make me say it, baby. Please, just give me what I need from you. I need it so bad."

I ran my helmet all around her clit, then put him into her hole. Teasing her, I pulled him back out. I needed to hear those words because I knew that the Pastor's wife was a boss freak just like me. Shit, she had turned me out a long time ago.

"Tell me, momma and, I'ma beat this pussy up like Vincent can't. I know you need yo' baby." I put the head back into her, held him there, then pulled him back out and laid him on her wet sex lips.

She moaned. "Okay, son, I love it. I love everything you do, and the fact that you touched her pussy, but still needed me. It makes me crazy. Now, please fuck me, baby. Do momma good. I need you so, so bad." She opened her eyes, and tears fell down her cheeks.

I leaned down and licked them away from her face, took my dick and slid it into her like a hot knife going into butter. Her walls sucked at me immediately. It felt like an inferno inside of her. I felt right at home with that grown pussy. I got to beating her kitty up, finding it even more hotter because my piece had just been inside of her daughter less than twenty minutes ago. That taboo shit was real for me.

"Harder, son! Harder, baby! Please! Unnnn! Yes! Harder, son! I need it harder! Unn! Unnn, yesss! I love! I love youu!"

My hips slammed into her again and again. I mean, I was trying to kill that pussy. The noises she made drove me nuts. Then, the fact that her and her daughter's cats smelled alike was also getting to me in a good way. It didn't take long before I was cumming deep within her. Afterwards, I held her in her marital bed while she told me how much she loved me and that I belonged to her and only her. I mean, she had to know that that wasn't true, but I didn't say nothing. I just rolled with it and allowed for her to pour her heart out.

She was a real simple and emotional woman. She wore her heart on her sleeve, and over the years I was able to learn her like the back of my hand. I think one of the many reasons why she cheated on the Pastor with me was because she secretly had a thing for young men. The Pastor had this way about making her feel old. His way of giving her a compliment was to say something like, "Wow, Vicki, you look good in that dress. But ten years ago, you looked even better." Or, he'd be like, "Baby, you better step your game up this Sunday, 'cause it's some young girls in that church that make me wanna break our vows." Then he'd laugh like that shit was cool or something. I'd caught her on more than one occasion crying after him giving her his version of a compliment.

Mrs. Jones was emotionally weak, and I felt like she just needed to hear on a regular basis that she was beautiful and desired by somebody like me, and that the world didn't end or begin with the Pastor's compliments.

So, after we got done getting it in, I held her in my arms, and kissed her on the forehead. "Momma, I hope you know that you are beautiful and that every day you get more and more fine to me. I don't want you thinking that just because me and Simone play around sometimes that it will take my love and desire away from you, because it never will. You're my heart, and I love you." I hugged her more firmly.

She turned on her side and wrapped her thick thigh around my waist. I could feel her hot pussy pulsating against my hip. "Thank you for saying that, baby. I really needed to hear it. As long as you love me, then I don't care what goes on. You're my baby, and you're the only one that makes me whole. Don't you ever forget that. I don't mind y'all playing around; just be safe and don't get that girl pregnant. I'm trusting you because I know I can't stop y'all from screwing around, but please keep both of your futures in mind. That and the fact that if Vincent finds out, he's going to kick you out of the house and probably even call the police. I don't want nothing like that happening to you, baby. I would literally die." She kissed my chest and rubbed all over my stomach muscles, before laying her head on my chest. "I love how your dick smells, baby. Uhh, everything about you just makes me looney."

She got to kissing on me again, but my mind was somewhere else. I was thinking about Purity and praying that she was okay. I had not checked in on her that morning, and now I was starting to regret that because I knew that daily she was going through hell with the Deacon and his family. I couldn't wait until I would be able to take her away from them.

A few moments later, Mrs. Jones jumped up to take a shower and invited me in, but I declined her offer. I'd had enough pussy for the morning. I was worn out. I went to my room and fell face first in the bed. Before I could adjust to a comfortable position, I was out like a light.

I couldn't have been sleep for more than three hours when I felt somebody pushing me again and again. It took me a while to open my eyes, but when I finally did, I saw Simone standing over me with a gun in her hand. I damn near had a heart attack. I got to thinking that she was finna pop me on some fatal attraction type shit. I sat up and scooted all the way back to the headboard, trying to figure out my next move.

"Shemar, you left this stuff in my room." She held up the pillowcase from the robbery. "It's two guns in here, and a whole bunch of money. What you done did? And whatever it is, I want some of this money since I'm yo' girl now," she whispered, then looked over her shoulder.

I exhaled loudly, and shook my head. The element of surprise was just starting to leave my brain. That and the cloudy feeling. Once I regained my common sense, I started to make some sense of things. I frowned, then scooted across the bed, taking everything from her, including my gun that she was

holding really awkward. I thought she was gon'
accidentally pull the trigger at any second.

"Simone, what you talking about you my girl? I
ain't ever said no shit like that. You my lil' sister.
That's all that's to it." I sat the pillowcase on my bed
before opening it up and looking inside of it. It was
still filled with bundles of cash, and the taped
package of what I assumed was dope. "You touch
any of my money in here?" I asked, looking at her
from the side of my face with my right eyebrow
raised.

She scrunched her face then crossed her arms
over her chest. "Boy, n'all. You know you ain't even
gotta ask me nothing like that. What you mean, I ain't
yo' girl? What? I ain't pretty enough or something?"
She sounded hurt and a little defeated.

I shook my head. "It ain't got nothing to do with
that. You been my lil' sister for how many years
now? Why all of a sudden you hollering this
girlfriend stuff?"

She sucked her teeth loudly. "So, you be doing
all that shit that we just did with Purity? Because if
that's how a brother and sister get down, then cool,
I'll just be yo' sister then. Long as we gon' keep on
doing us. Now, what about the money? I need some."
She gave me a stern look and held her hand out.

She was getting on my nerves. I didn't know
where her mother or father was, and I didn't like her
being in my room after what her mother had caught
us doing. I didn't care that she had basically given us
permission to play around, I still felt really odd with
her being in my room. At least until I could locate
her father.

"Aiight, how much you talking? I ain't got no problem with hitting yo' hand, because you deserve it. Just don't come at me with no outrageous number."

She smiled. "I just need a few hundred, just to have in my pocket for whatever. I hate being broke, and my daddy only gives me an allowance every other week." She stomped her small foot, and I noted that her toe nails were painted with white tips. She kept them boys well pedicured. To me, there was nothing like a female with some pretty toes. Her mother's were the same way.

I went into the pillowcase and peeled off five one hundred dollar bills and hit her with them. "Look, this you right here. Anytime you hurting or you need something, you let me know. You ain't always gotta depend on yo' daddy. I got you. You too bad to be walking around with no paper. A female is always supposed to have at least a few hundred on her at all times, so I'll make sure of that. You hear me?"

She shrieked, then ran to me and wrapped her arms around my neck, before kissing all over my lips, moaning into my face. After she broke the kiss, she backed up and looked me from head to toe. "I don't give a fuck what you talking about. I'm yo' girl now, and you gon' have to honor that. I'll do anything that you want me to do, and I'll compete with any female in them streets for you, because we supposed to be together. So, you can call me yo' sister, but we gon' break a whole lot of moral rules then. Oh, and I heard you with my momma. Y'all too much." She shook her head.

I simply grabbed her, and tongued her down again. I didn't feel like getting into a major discussion right then. I still had to break them pistols down and get rid of them, and find out what kind of dope was in the package. "Look, Simone, I got you. If you wanna mess with a nigga like me, knowing how I get down, and how close we grew up, then I'm with it. Just as long as you stay in yo' lane. And sooner or later, I'm gon' have to tame all of this." I gripped her ass, and pulled her back to me as she moaned into my ear.

Chapter 7

I had a whole kilo of heroin, and I was geeked up. Street value for a kilo of heroin in Houston was eighty thousand, and I intended on getting every penny of that. Me, Q, Nikki, and Tim sat in Nikki's trap, bagging up dime bags while they passed a blunt around. I ain't feel like smoking because I had so much shit on my brain. I was trying to figure out how I was gon' go at this heroin shit, because niggas were real selfish when it came to hustling in Houston. Mafuckas felt like if you weren't hustling under them, meaning paying them dues for every few hundred you made off of your own dope, then you weren't hustling in the hood period. I wasn't the type of nigga to pay nobody dues but seeing as how I had a whole kilo of dope, and Nikki had the same in order for us to hustle out in Cloverland, we had to pay somebody dues or get the nod from a higher up.

I was a stick-up kid. All that dope selling shit wasn't my cup of tea. To me, it was too slow. I usually preferred to let another cat do all of the hustling, and then I go hit his ass in one whop. But since me and Nikki were a lil' hot because of all of the murders, I had to find another way for a short while.

"Shemar, you quiet as a muthafucka homie. What's going on in that big ass head of yours?" Nikki asked, popping a Xanax pill. She had her hair in some short, tight Shirley Temples and it was making her look fine as hell. Even though she fucked with nothing but women, she was still a real fine, feminine female. Often times I had to take a double look at her.

She kept her hair, her nails and her toes done up, and even though she only wore make up every now and then, she was killing broads. I gave her about a nine over all. Only reason she ain't get that ten was because she was my homie, and ten meant I would have to go at her with everything that I had.

"I'm just ready to get this money, that's all." I foiled up another dime bag. "Who we finna get the nod from to be able to hit the market?" I asked, looking up at her as she put her hand on my shoulder. She smelled like Prada perfume.

"We gon' holla at Vito 'nem over on Middleton Road. My best friend used to fuck with him, and he's calling shots over there now. I'm pretty sure that he'll give us the go ahead. Once we get that, we'll be okay. We gon' meet with him later on today and see what it do." She rubbed my back. "Calm down, nigga. We gon' have that paper right before yo' birthday. I know what you trying to accomplish. We gon' get Purity. That's my word."

Even though I loved her to death when it came down to my sister, I didn't believe in nobody's word other than my own, because I knew I would make it happen for her with my life on the line. She was my everything. I was gon' hustle as hard as I could until my birthday, rather Nikki was beside me or not. "I know you got me Nikki, but I still gotta lead this ship."

She leaned over and kissed me on the cheek, then wiped it away with her thumb. "You know we in this shit together. I'll die before I let you fail."

After we spent a few more hours bagging up our work, we put a bundle in Tim and Q's hands and told them to hit the boulevard and get money. Nikki was sure that by the time we linked back up with them that we would have an official trap to hustle out of.

We jumped into my Chevy and headed over to Middleton. On the way, something was nagging at my heart, so as I pulled down my sun visor to block the bright ass sun, I got at Nikki about it.

"So, tell me what happened to Chelsey. You bodied her? I sho' ain't seen her on the news yet."

She lowered her window and sparked her blunt, taking a deep pull. "N'all, I ain't kilt her. We don't need too because she ain't gon' say shit." She reached and turned up the Yo Gotti song that was banging out of my speakers.

I turned that shit right back down because she had my heart thumping hard in my chest. I couldn't believe that she'd left a loose end that could murder us down the road. "Explain to me what you talking about, Nikki, and keep in mind that you gettin' me real heated right now. I expect more from you."

She let her seat all the way back and exhaled loudly. "Damn, sometimes you gotta trust me. I know Chelsey. That bitch ain't stupid enough to tell nobody what went down. Especially since she the one that put us on his line. She's an accessory to all of this shit. So how would that look?"

I accidentally rolled through a red light because I was mugging the shit out of her. A few cars blew their horns at me, and I was just lucky there wasn't no police around, or we would have been booked. "Nikki, ain't no such thing as an accessory to nothin' if shawty's ass was dead. Now, you quick to pull that trigger. Why all the sudden you're harboring feelings for this broad?"

She was quiet for a long time. "She pregnant, man, and I been knowing her since the second grade. That shit would kill me. I just don't know how to do it. Her daughter loves me, too."

I almost drove up on the sidewalk because I was looking at her for so long. I had never in my life heard her make excuses for why she couldn't kill somebody. She had been a part of the streets since her old man got killed. So many people had fucked her over and tried to take advantage of her, that her heart had turned colder than ice. I always knew that if I didn't have the strength to kill somebody, that she would. Now, she was folding over Chelsey? That was throwing me for a loop.

"Check this out, Nikki. After we holler at Vito, we're going over there and you gon' body shawty's, ass because that's how the game go. Ain't no way in hell we finna let one person be our downfall. It's too much shit at stake here. Whatever you feeling, get over that shit. I know you fucking that girl, but so what? It's plenty pussy out here, and its plenty niggas that I was in the second grade with that I'd knock they heads off with no remorse. Especially over you. This broad being alive is jeopardizing not only me and your lives, but Purity's as well. She gotta go. If you won't do it, I will." I curled my upper lip and shook my head in disgust.

She was quiet for a long time while Yo Gotti rapped in the background. She could tell that I was disappointed because she sat up and stubbed her blunt out in the ashtray. "Shemar."

I ignored her ass and kept on driving. I didn't wanna hold a conversation with her because I was afraid of what I might have said. Even though she was a goon at heart, she was still very emotional when it came to me.

"Shemar," she whispered with her voice breaking up. Once again, I ignored her. She laid her head on my shoulder. "Shemar, I'm sorry. You know I'll handle business. Don't be mad at me. You know I can't take that shit. You all I got in this world. Now, please, say something to me. I love you, big homie."

Even though I wanted to keep on rolling, I couldn't do her like that. I knew she was hurting, and the only person in this world that could truly heal her was me. I turned my head to the side and kissed her on the forehead. "I love you too, Nikki. You know I do, but they gon' treat us like adults. The state of Texas sending us to real prison now, which means that we gotta be ten times more careful. If we gon' be whacking muhfuckas, then we gotta make sure that all leads are burnt off. That's the way it gotta be. No mercy from here on out. We all we got. You hear me?"

She nodded while still on my shoulder. I could tell that she was emotional. "Shemar, I hate when you ignore me like that. You be making me feel like I'm all alone in this world, and that's scary. I hate when you get disappointed in me. I feel like shutting down. Did you know that?" she asked, picking her head up and looking into my face.

I kissed her on the lips. "I know. You tell me that all the time. That just mean you gotta step yo' game up, but I hate lettin' you down too. I don't give a fuck how many niggas or females you kill, you still just my lil' baby."

She smiled. "Shut up. I ain't always gon' be this soft over yo' ass. I hope you know that. You just, ugh, I don't know what it is, but you the only one that can get me here." She kissed my dimple, and then laid her head back on my shoulder while I drove to Middleton, banging Yo Gotti.

About thirty minutes later, Vito was slamming a domino down on the table. We sat around in his backyard, watching him play with a few of his niggas. Vito was about forty years old, yet still in real good shape. He had on a white beater that was tight as hell, but it showcased his ripped arms and tats. He had three dudes standing behind his chair with pistols on their hips, and they also wore white beaters. These niggas looked like they were fresh out the joint and still had an addiction to baby oil.

There was an above-ground pool in the backyard, and about ten thick ass females were going in and out of it. They wore G-strings that were basically pointless. Their tops were see-through, and I was having a hard time focusing on the task at hand.

One lil' red bone with a yellow bikini walked over to me and grabbed my hand. "Damn, playboy, you fine as hell with them green eyes and thangs. You got these muscles popping out everywhere. Why don't you get in the pool with me, so we can get to know each other a lil' better," she said, licking her lips.

Vito reached over and smacked her on the ass so hard that he made me jump. I watched it jiggle before it turned red. "Leah, get yo' ass in that house before

I fuck you up, with yo' lil' fast ass. Say, homie, don't pay my lil' sister no mind. She just trying my patience, and she only seventeen."

Leah mugged the shit out of him through her brown eyes. She rubbed her ass right in my face. I knew it wasn't intentional, but I didn't miss a beat. Them big globes kept on shaking every time she switched from one to the other. I could smell the chlorine coming off of her skin, mixed with the scent of perfume.

"Dang, you always hating on me. This nigga sitting here, fine as hell, and ain't none of these other hoes saying shit. I'm finna be eighteen in two weeks. You treating me like a kid, Vito!" She stomped her feet, and walked into the house with her G-string missing between her globes. As bad as she was, there was no way that I could have her walking around the house like she was without feeling some type of way.

I must've been peeping her too closely because Nikki bumped me with her elbow. "Shemar."

I jumped a lil' bit and tried to act like I wasn't peeping shawty as closely as I was.

Vito grunted, then raised his left eye brow. "Didn't you just hear me say that she only seventeen, lil' homie?"

I noticed that the niggas standing behind him were mugging me now. The sun shined off of their black foreheads. They looked like they were more angry than he was.

I shrugged. "I'm seventeen, too. Yo' sister bad, big homie. I ain't gon' front like she ain't, but I don't mean no disrespect, though."

He smiled and waved me off. "You good. I know how she look, but if you gon' be doing business with me, or you want my go ahead, you can't be fucking with nobody from my bloodline. That's how the game go. What you think about that?"

I was trying to get over the fact that he had her walking around in front of all of his niggas, damn near naked, yet he was making it seem like he wasn't with nobody messing with her on that level. Leah was built like a top-notch stripper. I felt like any man would look at her and get to lusting right away. At least, I know I did.

"I can respect that. For me, it's all about getting the money. So, how do we get yo' blessing into the game?"

Vito laughed. "You don't look like you no seventeen, and you carry yo' self like a grown man." He lit a cigarette and blew the smoke into the air. "Lil' Nikki say y'all got about seventy-two ounces of heroin; am I right?"

I nodded. "Somethin' like that. All we wanna do is hit the ground running and get this paper, because I got some stuff I gotta handle on my home front."

He nodded and pulled on the hairs of his chin. "Well, you already know that everything is run under structure out here in Cloverland. Even more so now that Hurricane Harvey came through and wrecked our city. Everybody trying to get they weight up, and it's a whole lot of anarchy going on that's getting muhfuckas' heads knocked off, 'cause we ain't honoring no shit like that. Am I right, homeboys?" He looked behind him at the men that were guarding his back. They laughed and agreed with him before he was looking back at me. "Y'all wanna serve that Boy then y'all gon' work in a trap that I set you up in, and my fee is sixteen thousand after both birds are pushed. That's ten percent off of each kilo. The trap I'ma put you in, you should make eighty gees a piece. Ten percent of eighty is eight, times that by two, and that's my take home— sixteen racks. You understand that?"

I understood everything he was saying, but I imagined myself losing out on eight stacks, and was about to get up and walk off on this big, black ass nigga. I wasn't with that shit, and I damn sure didn't wanna get caught up working for no nigga in Houston. I shook my head. "N'all, that shit don't sound right to me. I ain't giving up no sixteen gees for serving my dog food. You gotta come better than that, or offer me more of an incentive."

Once again, he laughed, and his niggas mugged me with hatred.

I didn't give a fuck. Far as I was concerned, this would be the last time I would be hollering at these niggas.

"Lil' nigga, where you from?"

"I'm from Damon, about twenty blocks from here. Land of the Trap."

He nodded. "Well, check dis out. This Cloverland, and I run these parts. It just so happens that Damon is in my territory, which mean you run under me. I want sixteen off them two birds, and you gon' work out of my Trap. That's the way shit gon' go, or I'ma send one of my hittas with you, and you just gon' turn over both birds, or he gon' hit both of yall. Now, how that sound?"

I stood up and grabbed Nikki's hand. "Look, bruh, I don't know you like that, but shit ain't sweet. You send a hitta to me, I'ma send you a body back. Ain't no bitch over here. Not even my lil' homie, right here," I said nodding my head at Nikki.

His niggas upped their pistols and aimed them at me and her, while Vito took a sip from his Orange Juice and smiled again.

I put Nikki behind me and mugged the shit out of all them niggas. "Nikki, go wait for me in the car. You don't need to be around this shit right now." I was sick because I had broken our pistols down and threw them into the river. Had I kept one of them, I would have made them kill me after Nikki went to the car.

She sucked her teeth and stood beside me. "N'all, fuck that, Shemar. These niggas smoke you, they gotta smoke me too. Like you said, ain't no bitch over here. Buss, niggas." She lifted her shirt and pulled out a .45 that I didn't even know she was carrying.

The females in the pool jumped out of it, and one by one, they ran into the house. I could hear them telling Leah what was going on outside.

Vito took a sip from his Orange juice again. "Lil' girl, you betta put that pistol up before you cause a world of trouble." He curled his upper lip and took another sip.

Nikki cocked the .45. "Look, Vito, it's clear that you ain't trying to honor what we on, so we'll just find another plug out of yo' territory. It is what it is."

Vito scrunched up his face and nodded. "Y'all get the fuck out of my backyard. Lucky for you two my lil' sister here, along with her girlfriends. But trust me, I'll be in touch. Cloverland ain't that big. Am I right fellas?"

They didn't say a word. They just kept on mugging me and Nikki. Had I had the .45 in my hand, I would have started bussing because these niggas looked grimy as hell. I already knew that we was finna have a whole lot of drama coming our way from them, and I felt like had they been dead already, we wouldn't have had to go through it.

"Let's go, Nikki, before shit get out of hand," I said, trying to remember each face that was in that backyard.

We slowly made our way out of there, keeping our eyes on them the whole time. As I was walking along the gangway, I looked up to the house and made eye contact with Leah, who was looking out of the window. I couldn't believe that she actually had the nerve to wave bye to me.

As soon as we got into my car, Nikki started to freak out. "Fuck, Shemar! I swear them niggas gon' be at our heads. I gotta switch my trap up. I already know how they get down. That nigga Vito is sheisty as fuck. He killed his own father for stealing an ounce of dope from him. Now we done flexed on they ass, and pulled a pistol on him and his niggas in his backyard. That definitely ain't finna ride with no consequences."

I knew she was right, but I was too irritated to give a fuck. I was trying to figure out why she'd thought dude was our best entrance into the game, especially since she was saying that he was sheisty and shit. "Why you pick that nigga, then? Why we ain't try to get in through somebody else?" I asked without even looking at her.

"Nah, nigga, don't blame that shit on me. We was good. You got to popping off at that nigga about his prices. Once you went down that road, I knew he was finna get heated and be on some fuck shit. I knew you wasn't finna honor it. Instead of me keeping my mouth closed, I'm letting it be known that I'm riding with you until the dirt. So, if they looking to body you, they might as well hit me, too." She grabbed the blunt out of the ashtray and lit it. "Fuck, my high is blown."

I knew we couldn't stand for no drama at that time, especially since we were on the clock to get our paper in order. Well me, especially, but I just couldn't see myself letting no nigga squeeze me for my chips. "Man, I say we sell both them birds and keep pulling these kick-doors to get our paper right. I sho' ain't about to be sitting in no trap, catching that slow ass money, and be worried about the police and these punk ass niggas."

She coughed and hit herself in the chest with her fist while she leaned forward. "I agree. Let's just get rid of that dope and keep on doing what we do best. On some real shit, though, we might need to consider smoking dude ass. My nerves too bad to be wondering about when he gon' strike. So, we gotta figure that shit out."

"You know what? I agree."

Chapter 8

The next night, me and Nikki was sitting in front of one of the homies from the hood, named Ace. He was a real skinny, dark skinned, tall nigga with long dreads and a mouth full of gold. In our part of Cloverland, he was well-respected. I didn't know how he felt about Vito and I didn't ask. J. Prince was supposed to be his uncle. I didn't know if that was true or not, but what I did know was that he had plenty bread. Me and Nikki had considered hitting him a few times but had never got around to doing it. I think we were both low key a lil' afraid because Ace had some true Goons running under him.

We sat in his den, with the big screen television playing the movie "Belly" behind us. He leaned his head forward and tooted up a thick line of heroin that we were trying to sell to him. "Aww! That's some good shit right there. Yeah, I feel them effects already," he said, pinching his nose and scratching his shoulder. Then, he sat down across from us on a love seat. He was dressed in Versace pajamas and slippers. He closed his eyes and smiled.

I looked at Nikki and she looked back at me. She had the look of confusion on her face, and I was confused as well. Two bodyguards stood on each side of the door of the den. They looked like they weighed three hundred pounds apiece.

"So, what you think, Ace? You want it?" I asked, growing impatient. The Pastor was having some sort of revival at the church, and he was saying that I had to be there to help serve meals afterwards.

I didn't know why he insisted on me being there, but I knew I had to.

"I'll give you a hundred gees fa both keys. In cash. Right now," he said without opening his eyes. He continued to scratch his shoulder.

I also noted that even though he looked clean, he smelled like funk. I was trying my best to not inhale this nigga, because it was getting to my stomach.

I shook my head. "N'all man, I can get eighty apiece for this shit. Why you low balling me?" I asked, getting ready to get up.

"Aiight, seventy apiece, but I can't go no higher than that right now. It's all the cash that I got here, so you gotta take it or leave it." He opened his eyes and sat forward in his seat, looking at me with yellow eyes.

That meant that we would be leaving twenty bands on the table. We had just left an offer on the table with Vito that would have left us with sixteen bands left on the table. He was asking to keep an additional four. I wasn't cool with that.

I guess Nikki saw that I was finna say somethin' slick so she spoke up. "Look, Ace, if we take that hundred and forty, what's good with some firearms? We need some pistols to bark at a few niggas if the heat get on. What you got in that department?" she asked, looking him over closely.

He smiled and sat back in his love seat. "What kind you talking about? Revolvers or semi-autos?"

"We leaving twenty bands on the table. Why don't you throw us a whole lil' package together and we can call it even tonight," I said, watching him shake as if he had the chills or something. Before we left, that's exactly what he did.

We got back to Nikki's Trap and bussed down everything that he had given us. We had enough work to protect ourselves for the moment. He'd even thrownin a few fully automatics to knock some niggas on they ass, with a bunch of ammunition. I was grateful she had spoken up, because I would have ruined everything since I felt like he was trying to play us at first.

After I filled up my duffle bag that I was gon' hide in my storage locker at the Pastor's house, I gave Nikki a hug. "Look, I love you, girl. Get you some sleep so we can be up bright and early in the morning. We gotta check in on Tim 'nem, and see what that Loud situation looking like. We good though. We just sold nearly two keys, minus what we gave Tim 'nem, and we came up on hella money and pistols. Tomorrow is a new day."

She hugged me then stood on her tippy toes and kissed me on the cheek. "I love you too, and I'll see yo' crazy ass in the morning."

I made my way outside as I heard her lock the door. My car was parked in the back of her house, in the alley. I made my way through her backyard, got to my car, opened the trunk, and sat the duffle bag in it when the gunshots went off in a rapid fashion.

Boom-boom-boom-boom-boom-boom! Boo-wa! Boo-wa! Boo-wa! Boom-boom-boom-boom-boom-boom-boom-boom-boom! Boo-wa! Boo-wa! Boo-war!

I ducked down and opened the door to my car. At first, I didn't know where the shots were coming from until it hit me. Nikki's trap was being shot up. And when I say shot up, I mean it was

getting rocked like crazy. Luckily, I had loaded up one of the .40 Glocks and put it on my hip before I'd left her trap. I slammed the door to my car and ran back into her backyard at full speed until I got to her backdoor, while the shots continued to sound off in front of the house loudly.

Boom-boom-boom-boom-boom-boom-boom!
Boo-wa! Boo-wa! Boo-wa!

I kept my back to the back door, then ran to the gangway and looked to the front of the house. I saw two vans parked in the middle of the street with their side doors opened. As the shots rang out, I could see the fire spitting from the barrels of their guns. I felt my heart thumping in my chest. My adrenalin got to pumping. I imagined one of the bullets hitting Nikki, and I lost it. I ran down the gangway bussing my gun again and again.

Boom! Boom! Boom! Boom! Boom! I was aiming right at the side door where the armed men were shooting. *Boom! Boom! Boom!* One fell out of the van and onto his back in the street. One of the vans stormed away, and then I saw two dudes with half masks on their faces running off of her porch and into the van that the one dude had fallen out of. I bussed my gun again, trying to knock one of their heads off. Boom! Boom! One of the dudes jerked and turned around before falling against the van. The other dude jumped over him and into the vehicle as it started to drive away. He must've saw me because he aimed his Tech .9 at me and squeezed the trigger. *Boom-*

boom-boom! Boom-boom-boom! Boom-boom-boom!

I ducked down and fell against the house for a brief second, then bussed again as the van stormed down the street with the dude that I had hit falling out of the side door. I ran full speed until I got into the middle of the street where he was squirming on the pavement, with his face scrunched in pain.

Blood oozed out of his mouth and dripped off of his chin. I could tell that he was choking on his own blood. I had visions of shooting him straight in the face, but then I heard sirens off in the distance. That made me take off running.

I got to the back of Nikki's house and beat on the door. "Nikki! Nikki! Open up, ma! Dem fuck niggas gone! Come on, now!" I waited for a few second with no response, and then I got to panicking because I was remembering how the front of the house looked. It looked like they had pumped a minimum of two hundred shots into her crib.

I got worried. I needed Nikki. She was my heart. I couldn't see myself grinding in them streets without her. She was my right hand's diamond.

I beat on the door again. "Nikki! Open the door, ma! Please!"

The sirens got closer, and I got more and more worried.

Finally, the door opened and Nikki fell into my arms. "Shemar, them bitch ass niggas shot me, homie. Here. Grab this shit, and let's go." She flung her duffle bag at me, and I put it over my left shoulder while I helped her out of the house, guiding her with my right arm.

"Where are you shot?" I asked, feeling sick on my stomach. I couldn't believe this shit was happening. I was wishing it could have been me and not her. I didn't give a fuck how hard she was, she was still a female and it was my job to protect her at all times. I felt like I had failed her.

"In my back and in my shoulder over here. Don't worry about it. Just get me in the car and let's get the fuck away from here," she said in a raspy voice.

I blinked tears as I helped her into the backseat of my car, just as the police slammed on their brakes in front of her trap. There had to be at least six of them. The lights on top of their cruisers lit up the neighborhood.

As soon as I had her situated in the back, I kissed her on the forehead and then the lips. "You gone be okay, Nikki. I swear I got you, or I'll die right beside you tonight. That's on my mama," I said, feeling the tears run down my cheeks.

I got behind the wheel, started the car, and peeled out of the alley. I came to where the alley met the street and made a right turn onto a side street. Two police cars flew past us, on their way to the scene of the shooting. I was worried that they were going to get behind us if I didn't get out of that area. I made another right, then a left onto Martin Luther King Drive, and jumped on the highway, taking my whip to maximum speeds.

"You okay back there, Nikki? Let me know somethin', momma?"

"This shit hurt, Shemar. It's killing me, big homie. I need you, man. I need you to make this pain stop. Please!" I could hear her groaning behind me, and then the sniveling started.

I had a heavy heart for her. I wished that we could trade places. "Look, Nikki, I love you, baby, and you know you strong enough to pull through. I gotta get you to Clark county, where they finna pull them slugs out of you and stitch you right up. Then, we gon' go at them niggas. I know it ain't nobody but Vito 'nem bitch ass. You know they gotta pay for this shit. Right?" I looked into my rear-view mirror and saw that Nikki was struggling to keep her eyes open.

For the first time, I was able to make out the blood seeping out of her shoulder. The entire front of her Prada blouse was saturated. She coughed, and then closed her eyes.

"Nikki, holla at me. You can't fall asleep, momma. You got to keep on fighting. You know I need you now."

She fluttered her eyes, and then they rolled into the back of her head. I felt my heart drop, and then she started to convulse. "Arrgh! Arrrgh! Shemar, help me."

I stepped on the gas, pushing the car to the limit. I was growing scared out of my mind. I needed to get her to the hospital where they could save her life. I knew that she was losing a lot of blood, and due to the fact that she was only about a hundred and twenty pounds, she didn't have much blood to lose.

It usually took me about fifteen minutes to get to Clark County from Cloverland, but this night, I got there in five. I slammed on the brakes in front of the hospital, threw my whip in park, and opened the back door before slowly placing my arms under Nikki, and lifting her out of the car. She felt heavier than usual, and she was covered in blood. I couldn't stop the tears from falling from my eyes. It was my job to protect her, and I had been ever since we'd been kids. At this crucial time in life, I had failed her.

"Hold on, baby. I swear to God, I love you so much. Please hold on." The automatic door opened and I ran inside of the hospital with her. "Help me! Please! Somebody, help me! She has been shot!" I wailed before laying her on the nurses' station counter.

The white woman looked up at me with big eyes before picking up the phone and calling on some help.

When they took her out of my arms, I fell to my knees and broke all the way down. I got to imagining the worst, and in my heart I knew I wasn't strong enough to accept it. The bottom line was that I needed Nikki. I loved Nikki, and she was my heart. I knew that when it was all said and done, I was finna make Vito and all of his niggas pay, one way or the other.

Chapter 9

I had to get out of the hospital before the police came and tried to question me. I had so much shit in my car that it would have landed me in prison for a long time. So, even though I didn't want to leave Nikki's side, I knew that I had to or it would have costed us way more than we were willing to pay.

Before I got to the Pastor's house, I called Mrs. Jones and told her to meet me outside of the house because I needed to talk to talk to her about something very important. That night, when I pulled up, the porch lights came right on, and she stepped out of the house with a light jacket pulled close around her.

She came all the way to my car, and opened the passenger's door. As soon as the interior light came on she must've saw all of the blood because she freaked out. "Oh my God, son, what happened to you?" she asked, grabbing me to her.

I laid my head on her chest and allowed for the tears to run out of my eyes. "It ain't me, momma, it's Nikki. She got shot tonight, and I couldn't do nothing to help her. It's all my fault. I don't know what to do."

She rubbed my back and hugged me tighter. "Baby, it's going to be okay. Momma is here now. Just tell me what happened."

I was so sick, remembering how Nikki felt in my arms with the blood pouring out of her, that I couldn't even think straight enough to get the words out. I tried the best I could.

After hearing what took place, I felt her hug me tighter. "I'm so glad that it wasn't you, Shemar. I don't know what I would do if it had been you, baby. I love you so, so much. You're my everything. I mean that."

Though her words helped some, all I could think about was Nikki. I wondered if she had pulled through, and if so, if she was still in pain. I was hoping that she was resting because I didn't want her to wake up and not see me by her side. I just wanted to hold her in my arms. I wanted to protect her. I wanted to save her from the world of pain. Never again would I allow for anything to happen to her. I would be her protector with my life on the line, just as if she were Purity.

"Momma, I need for you to ride out to Clark County and claim to be her aunt. That way, when she wakes up, you can take her away. Please. I can't let her wind up back in the system. She don't turn eighteen for six months. That's too long."

Mrs. Jones shook her head. "Okay, baby, don't worry. I'll go get my keys and fly out there. You just take yourself into the house and wash this blood off of you. Then, get some rest, even though I know that's easier said than done."

I was so distraught and exhausted that I couldn't even put up a fight. I nodded. "Just promise me that you'll go get her."

She did.

After she left, I took all of the stuff out of my car, brought it into the house, and down to the basement, locking it away in my storage area. Then, I jumped in the shower, and on my way back to my room, I ran into the Pastor. He was coming out of his and Mrs. Jones' bedroom with his boxers on and shirt off.

The first thing he did when he saw me was shake his head. "And where were you tonight, young man?" he asked, squeezing past me in the hallway.

I had the bloody shirt and pants balled up; one on each hand. "Something came up. I wanted to be there, I just couldn't make it. I apologize, sir." I didn't feel like getting into a long talk with him. My mind was too cloudy for that. I just wanted to be alone and think things through. I needed to formulate my next move.

"Apology not accepted. Now when I tell you to do something, you're supposed to do it. You ain't eighteen yet, and you still live under my roof. So, since you can't obey my simple commands, you're going to clean this house from top to bottom before you go to sleep tonight. Do I make myself clear?"
I swear I wanted to snap out at this man, but I knew I had to keep my composure. He was only disciplining me in his own way. Everything that had taken place that night wasn't his fault. So, even though looking at his pot belly and his hairy chest irritated me more than you could imagine, especially since I wasn't in the mood for that shit, my only response was to nod. "Alright, I'll take care of it, sir."

He continued to make his way down the hall and into the bathroom that I had come out of. I knew he was getting ready for work.

You see, I never really had a problem with the Pastor. I just was who I was. His wife and his daughter were too hard to resist and I couldn't help that. I knew I was betraying him in a sense, but for the most part, I didn't harbor any real love for the man, or any man for that matter. At least not at that time.

Simone opened her door as soon as the bathroom door closed. "Psst! Psst! Shemar, come here," she whispered, stepping part way into the hallway in some pink boy shorts that were all up in her crease. Her caramel thighs were exposed and looked shiny and thick as ever. Even in my state of sorrow I couldn't ignore that fact, but I had to try.

I turned around and walked up to her. "Look, Simone, I'm sick right now and I can't talk," I whispered.

She looked hurt. Her face lowered and then she stuck out her bottom lip. "Dang, what did I do to you for you to avoid me like this?" She stepped further into the hallway and tried to hug me, but I stepped out of her grasp.

I wanted to get into my room so I could call Mrs. Jones to see how Nikki was doing, then I was gone wait for the Pastor to leave so I could burn them clothes in the incinerator. I exhaled loudly. "Simone, we good, baby. I swear it ain't got nothing to do with you. I'm just going through something right now, and I need to clear my head."

She nodded. "Well, I heard him tell you that you had to clean the house from top to bottom, so I'm just gon' do it for you because that's my place. I was just coming out my room to let you know that."

She looked so sick that I couldn't help myself from grabbing her and kissing her lips, stepping into her bedroom while I tongued her down, and she moaned into my mouth. I had already saw the effects of one female being hurt that night, I couldn't allow for it to be two.

So, I rubbed all over her ass and ended my kiss by sucking all over her thick lips. "Look, baby, I appreciate that. Soon as I get my head together, me and you gon' spend some time together. I promise."

She hugged me again and laid her head on my chest. "Ooh, I can't wait. I'ma prove some thangs to you. I love you so much."

I held her for a few moments longer, then released my arms from around her. It did feel good to hear her say that she loved me, because in that moment I had no love for myself. I felt defeated and sick as ever. Even the kiss that usually made me feel some type of way, this time I felt barely anything. That told me that I needed to be alone.

"Aiight. Baby, look, just handle that business for me, and I'll thank you later in any way that you need me too. I appreciate you. I hope you know that."

She smiled, then bit on her bottom lip all sexy like. "Well, I hope you feel better. I wish I could heal you in some way, but I'm just gon' give you your space. Have a good night, and remember that I really do love you."

I watched her walk out of the room and close the door, then I laid on my bed and tried to clear my mind as best as I could, but it was just impossible. Every time I tried to close my eyes, I saw the image of the blood rushing out of Nikki's body. I saw the pain written across her face. It started to make me more and more sick on the stomach.

Finally, I got up and texted Purity and told her that I was gon' meet her around the corner from her house in half an hour. Before I left, I threw the bloody clothes into the incinerator in the basement, and watched them burn up. Then, I left out of the back door and ran down the alley until I met Purity at our usual meeting place.

When I got there, she was already there, dressed in a pink and white Prada cheerleading fit, with the matching book bag. Her hair was freshly done, and she was rocking Prada shades that set her fit off. I loved seeing my lil' sister crushing shit on the dressing side. It made me feel like I was handling my business the way I was supposed to be.

When she saw me, she dropped her bag to the ground and ran to me at full speed before she crashed into me and wrapped her arms around my neck, holding me tight. I held her just as firm, and for about two minutes we didn't say anything to one another. We were lost in time.

Finally, I felt a few raindrops falling from the sky. I decided to break the silence. "I missed you lil' sis. I swear I have."

She laid her head on my chest and exhaled, then shook her head. "I can't wait for this to be over. I can't wait until we never have to worry about being separated again. This is really killing me. I need you, big bruh."

I took a step back and looked her over closely. I felt my throat get real tight, and I just needed to release my emotions into her. I felt like I was on the verge of breaking down, and she must've sensed that.

She put her little hands up to my face and held it. "What's the matter? Why do you look so sick?" Her stare was that of concern. Her eyes were big, and she swallowed more than once as if she was getting choked up before I even told her what the matter was.

The rain was corning down a lot harder now, but we acted like it didn't even exist, until finally she flipped open her umbrella.

I stepped under it as the thunder roared in the sky. "Nikki got shot up, and I don't know if she gon' make it or not. I don't know what to do, but I think I'm losing my mind, Purity."

Her eyes got as big as paper plates. She looked shocked. "Oh my God. Where did this happen? Where did she get shot at?" She stepped forward and hugged me again, slightly taking the umbrella away so that the rain splattered against my forehead.

I adjusted it and hugged her back. "Some niggas aired her crib out, and she wound up getting hit in the back and shoulder. She lost a lot of blood, and I'm just losing my mind because I should have been there to protect her. Them niggas wet her crib up as soon as I left out of it. Fuck, this shit killing me." I felt like I wanted to slump to the ground. I didn't understand how much I cared about Nikki until she got hit with them slugs. Once again, I wished it would have been me instead of her.

Purity kissed my cheek. "Shemar, it's not your fault. You can't save everybody. You know had you been there that it would have never happened to her, but you had already left. Just be thankful that it didn't happen to you, because what good would that have been for us? Huh?" She exhaled loudly and rubbed tears away from my cheeks. "Nikki is a fighter. She's going to be okay. You just have to pray on it and leave it in God's hands. Be thankful that he didn't already take her life, and understand that if it was meant for her to go that she would have been dead already. For now, your focus should be on getting yourself together so you can be in the best possible shape when your birthday comes, because I want out of the Deacon's house. I'm at my wits end. I'm losing my mind in there, and I need you. Please don't do anything stupid over this. We're so close. I feel like it's the Devil that's trying to detour our plans, and we can't let that happen. No weapons formed against us shall prosper. Remember that saying?"

I lowered my head. "Yeah, I do." I was hearing everything that she was saying and it was making sense, but at the same time, my heart was killing me because of Nikki. In that moment, I didn't know what I was going to do, but I did know that I wasn't about to accept what happened to her without handling my business on her behalf.

After kissing my sister again, and watching her get on her school bus, I jogged back to the Pastor's house, locked myself in my room where I attempted to get my head together. Then, I got a disturbing text from Mrs. Jones telling me to meet her at the hospital. I damn near had a heart attack.

Chapter 10

I got there about an hour later. Mrs. Jones was waiting for me in the front of the hospital at the entrance. When she saw my car, she ran out into the rain until she got to me, then opened my passenger's door and got in. She looked rough. She had washed away her make up, and I could tell that she had been crying a lot. Her and Nikki had had a strong relationship ever since I had been living with her family. They often went out together, and Nikki even called her mom. The fact that she looked like she had been crying only added to my worry.

I felt like I was ready to break down. "Look, momma, just give it to me straight. Don't sugar coat nothing. What's going on with her?" I asked, pulling into the hospital parking lot, finding a space and parking there.

She swallowed and then blinked tears. "Son, she lost a lot of blood, and you did the best that you could to get her here on time, but sometimes God has a better plan for his children." She said this, and a string of clear snot came out of her nose onto her lip.

I blinked tears. "Momma, what is you saying, because I know you ain't saying what I think you is? Now, tell me what's good with Nikki or I'm finna go in there and find out myself. Tell me!" I hollered, feeling myself getting ready to lose all control.

She jumped, then lowered her head. "She's on life support, baby, but they're saying that she might not make it out of the week. I'm sorry."

Soon as she said it, my head fell forward and tears got to coming out of my eyes. I felt like I couldn't breathe. I opened my car door and fell to the ground in the pouring rain, on my knees, and cried my eyes out. I tried to imagine Nikki dying and I just couldn't take it. I couldn't see myself in a world without her. We had been as thick as thieves ever since we understood what a pistol was. Just her and me. Me and her. Us. Nikki and Shemar. So, I rocked back and forth on my knees until I started to throw up with the rain beating against my back. By this time, it was coming down so hard that it felt like hail.

Mrs. Jones got out of the car and knelt on the side of me, rubbing my back. "It's okay, son. You have to fight. We have to believe that she's going to pull through. it's all we have. We have to cast our cares upon Him, and allow for Him to take the wheel."

I cried and cried until I felt like I was about to pass out. Only then did I calm down enough to say a few words to Mrs. Jones. "Ma, I gotta see her. I gotta kiss her so she can get stronger. All she will need is my kisses. Trust me on this. Don't nobody know her like I do. We live for each other. If I can kiss her just one time, she'll get better, I promise."

I didn't know if that would actually happen, but I needed to see Nikki. I was feening for her. I needed to feel her skin again. To plant a kiss on her. I needed to be in the same room with my best friend. My right-hand woman.

Mrs. Jones nodded. "Okay, baby, we'll go in, but under no circumstances do you tell them who you are, and if they ask you if you know anything about what happened to her, you tell them no. You're simply my son, and she's your cousin. That's that.

Since you're a minor, they can't question you without my consent, so you just let me handle all of the talking if anyone from Law enforcement tries to accost you. You got that?"

I did, and that's what I told her.

Fifteen minutes later, I was walking into Nikki's room in the intensive care unit. As soon as I stepped foot inside and saw her laid on the bed on her side with a thick tube down her throat, and all kinds of machines hooked up to her body, I broke into another fit of tears. I didn't even know I had it in me to cry so much, but she was my heart. If it's one understanding that you get from this true story, you must get that. Nikki, alongside my sister, was my everything.

I ran over to the bed, and laid my face onto her soft cheek, while the machines beeped over and over again in the background. I could hear the air from the fat tube that was stuffed down her throat as clear as day. I raised my head and kissed her on the cheek.

Mrs. Jones stepped into the room and closed the door behind her. "They say we only got ten minutes, baby, so please do what you have to, but make it quick," she said, then sat on the couch a safe distance away.

I kissed Nikki on the forehead and rubbed her curly hair out of her beautiful face, stroking her cheek with my thumb. "Nikki, I know you're in there, Momma, and I just wanna let you know that I love you, and that I know you're going to pull through all of this. They only giving you a week, baby, but I know better. Don't nobody know you like I do," I said with my voice breaking up. I swallowed, and wiped another tear away. I kissed her again on the cheek, and stroked her hair. For a second, I looked at the machines and tried to read them unsuccessfully. I tilted my head back and took a deep breath, then looked back down on her. "Nikki, you're my heart, and I love you with all that I am. I need you, baby. I swear to God, I need you like never before. I can't make it in this world without my right hand. I'm handicapped without you, ma. You keep me strong. So, what I need for you to do is fight through this battle and get back to me so I can protect you and cherish you every single day, for the rest of my life. I promise to never allow for you to reach harm again. That's my word." I kissed her cheek again, then laid my face against hers until the machines started going haywire.

There was the loud sound of *Derrrrrrrrrrrrr!* Then, another machine started screeching loudly. I jumped back as the door flew open, and about four nurses and a doctor ran inside in a frenzy, bumping me out of the way.

"I'm sorry, sir, but you have to leave the room. Both of you," a black nurse said, pointing to the exit.

The nurses behind her started to check Nikki's neck, while another looked at the monitors. The doctor put on blue latex gloves, and pulled out a scalpel.

Mrs. Jones came from behind me and put her arm around my neck. "Come on, baby, let them take care of her," she cooed into my ear.

I reluctantly allowed for her to pull me out of the room. "Momma, just tell me that she gon' be okay. Tell me that she gon' be okay, momma. Please." I begged.

After she got me into the hallway, she wrapped her arms around me and held me while I tried to make sense of life in that moment.

Before we left the hospital, we were told that the medical team was able to bring her back to life again. That she remained on life support and that they would do everything that they could to keep her around, as long as possible.

That night, the Pastor found out what had happened to my best friend and he decided to come into my room to relay his empathy in his own way, but when it was all said and done, all he did was piss me off more.

He knocked on my door, and before I gave him permission to come in, he barged in and had the nerve to sit on the edge of my bed, while I laid with my head on the pillow, looking up at the ceiling. "Shemar, I heard about what happened to Nikki, and I wanna say I'm sorry about it. That's just how life goes when you ain't in the church. You can't be doing only God knows what in the streets and then don't think that the Devil won't strike when he gets good and ready to. You play on his playground, and he can throw sand in your face whenever he wants to. that's just how it goes. But you have my condolences, and I hope it taught you a lesson." He stood up and adjusted his cufflinks. "You wanna come to the church with me tonight, and we can pray for your friend?"

I had already been praying a million different prayers in my head. The last thing I needed was for a bunch of people that didn't even know Nikki to be saying prayers for her that they didn't really mean. At least that's how I felt. I shook my head. "N'all. I just wanna stay in my room and get my mind together, if that's okay with you, sir."

He nodded. "That's perfectly fine. I'll be out a little late tonight anyway. I got a few errands to run after service, so it's probably for the best. Far as the punishment goes, don't you worry about that. You just get yourself together, and whatever you need, you let your mother know. She's in the kitchen, cooking. Your sister is in her room, studying. They'll be there for you. Okay?"

"Thank you, sir. Drive safely, and keep Nikki in your prayers. She needs them right now."

"Will do." He stepped out of my room and closed the door. Five minutes later, I heard him backing out of the driveway.

I was missing Nikki like crazy, and the more and more I envisioned her laying in the bed, hooked up to all of those machines, the more I felt my heart turning cold. I knew I was finna fuck Vito and all of his niggas over; females and all if I had to. My main thing was that I wanted to torture his ass and make him feel ten times as much pain as Nikki was.

There was a soft knock on my door, and then Simone peeked her head in. "Big bruh, you okay? Do you want some company for a little while, to take your mind off of things?" she asked, with some cute Dolce and Gabbana reading glasses on. She looked real good, and I think that's why I said what I said.

"Yeah, come on in and close the door. I could use a lil' healing, because right now, my thoughts getting the best of me."

She smiled and stepped into my room, wearing a pair of real small, white biker shorts, with a tank top on that revealed she wasn't wearing a bra. I could make out both of her areolas, clear as day.

She came over and sat on the bed next to me, before leaning down and kissing my lips. "It's gon' be okay, big bruh. I got you. I know you need me to heal you right now, and that's what I'm here for." She sucked on my lips, then trailed her hand downward until she was gripping my dick in her little hand.

I was wearing Polo boxers, so she was feeling all of me.

I took her hand and put it inside of them. I wanted to feel her hand on my piece. I needed to take my mind off of Nikki. I didn't care if Mrs. Jones was in the kitchen. I needed to be healed. I had to be. My dick got hard instantly. She pulled it through my boxer's hole and stroked it, while I rubbed all over her soft, plump ass, until I was playing in her crease from the back.

"Umm, big bruh, there you go again, playing with my pussy. You want me to put this in my mouth, to show you how I been practicing?" She licked her lips, then leaned down and kissed my head, before tonguing it and sucking it into her mouth, while her fist pumped my whole pipe.

"Ummm, shit." I groaned deep within my throat, then squeezed her thick pussy lips together with my fingers. I could already feel her juices seeping through the fabric. Her crease felt hot, and I could smell her already. "Simone, pull them shorts down so I can play with that naked pussy. Let big bruh see what you working with again."

She let out a loud smacking sound as she popped my dick out of her mouth, and leaned over. It rested against her cheek while she pulled her biker shorts down her thighs half way, and left them there. Now, the scent of her pussy was loud as hell and it intoxicated me. To me, there was nothing like the smell of pussy. I loved it.

I picked her all the way up and sat her pussy on my mouth, while she grabbed a hold of my pipe, stroking him. Then, she sucked him back into her mouth, spearing her head on him again and again, slurping loudly.

"Huhhhh, Shemar," she whimpered as I peeled her brown lips apart, exposing her clit.

I sucked on it as if I was trying to nurse. I grabbed that big ass and forced her to hump into my face while I sucked on her clit and licked up and down her crease. I was tongue-fucking her tight hole, sucking all over her sex lips, all nasty like.

She sat up on my face and got to rocking back and forth, with her face pointed toward the ceiling. "Unn! Unn! Ummmhmm! Shemar. Umm! I love. I love you so much. Ummmmhmmm!" She rode my tongue faster and faster while her juices poured out of her and ran down my cheeks.

I gripped her ass even more and continued to slurp and suck. Her taste was driving me insane.

She gripped my dick and started pumping it real fast while she rode my tongue. I slipped two fingers up her hole and got to running them in and out of her at full speed. That made her hips buck faster. The springs on my bed were going haywire.

"Unn! Unn! I'm cumming, Shemar! Shemar! I'm! Cummmiiingggg!" She moaned and got to riding my face faster than she ever had before.

I could feel her juices squirting up against my nose and top lip. I continued to suck on her berry, tasting her and growing obsessed with her flavor.

Then, she hopped off of me, and bent over the bed. "Fuck this. I want that dick. I want yo' dick in me, right now. I need it. I don't care if I'm pose' to be yo' lil' sister. I want you to fuck me. Now, Shemar!" She leaned on to her stomach and opened her sex lips with two fingers.

Seeing her pink excited me. Nikki kept on flashing into my head, and I was trying my best to push her out for the moment. I needed some release. I needed to escape for a little while or I was going to go insane.

I hopped out of the bed and got behind her. I rubbed all over her fluffy ass cheeks. I smacked her on the left one, and took my dick head and ran it up and down her slit. My dick was as hard as a brick wall. The head slid through her lips with ease. It felt real hot and moist. I was going to slowly ease him into her, but then she slammed back into me and took my whole dick, all the way to my balls.

"Uhhh! Shit! It's in. It's in. Now, fuck me, Shemar. Fuck me like a gangsta. Please." She smashed her ass into my lap, leaned forward, and smashed it back again.

That was all I could take. I grabbed her hips and got to fucking her like I had been wanting to, ever since I was a young teen. Every time I pulled her back to me, I pumped my hips forward and attacked that tight pussy like I was mad at her.

She looked over her shoulder at me with her mouth wide open. Then, she ran her tongue across her lips, before biting into her bottom one. The curls on her head bounced up and down while I attacked her, making that ass vibrate. "Umm! Umm! Yes! Shemar! I love you! I love you, bruh! I'm yo' girl! I'm yo' girl! Umm, shit! Fuck lil' sis!" She then whimpered.

I pushed her face into the bed and got to really wearing that ass out. Her pussy was sucking at my pipe as if it was trying to pull it off of me. It was so good. Too good, that I got to cumming in her at the same time she got to cumming on me. "Ugh! Ugh! Ugh! Shit, Simone. I can't help it. I'm cumming. Shiiittt!" I slammed into her and unloaded again and again. My abs tightened and then released themselves.

"I'm cumming, big bruh. I'm cummmiiinnnggg!" She got to shaking so bad that I almost fell out of her. But I held on to them hips and kept on going like a Cowboy.

I felt two hands rub my back, and that caused me to jump and look over my shoulder. Mrs. Jones smiled, took the straps of her gown and pulled them off of her shoulders, before dropping her gown to the floor and stepping out of it. "You already know momma gotta heal you, too. You're my baby, and can't nobody heal my baby like I can." She kissed my lips, and we got to tonguing each other down while my dick was still in her daughter from the back. I could feel her walls vibrating and sucking at me.

Mrs. Jones pulled my dick out of Simone, dropped to her knees, and stroked him while looking up at me. Then, she popped him into her mouth and got to sucking me like she was try in to get me to marry her.

Simone started sucking on my neck and reaching over my shoulder to rub my chest. "That shit feel good, don't it, Shemar? We just gotta heal you. That's what momma said. She said that only we can heal you, and that's what we gon' do." She turned my head so she could suck on my lips.

We were tonguing like crazy while Mrs. Jones sucked my dick like a porn star. I was so caught off guard that I couldn't even get my thoughts in order. Everything was feeling so good. I had two bad females in the room with me, getting down like savages, and my body was going nuts.

Mrs. Jones licked all under my dick, and sucked each ball. "I know you finna turn eighteen, Shemar, but momma don't want you to leave us. If you can have me and Simone every day, would you stay with us?" Mrs. Jones asked, before popping me back into her mouth.

I felt her nip at my dick head with her teeth, and that caused me to cringe. It felt so good that I had tears in my eyes. "Damn, momma. That feel so good."

Simone rubbed her titties on my back. I could feel the hard nipples poking at me. "Don't forget about me, Shemar. I want you to stay, too. You're my big brother. Right?" She sucked on my neck, and rubbed her pussy against my lower back.

Mrs. Jones pushed me all the way back on the bed, then straddled me with her titties bobbing up and down on her chest. Both of her nipples were standing out at least an inch. She reached under herself and grabbed my dick, pulling the skin back, before sliding him into her super-hot and wet hole. "Uhhhhh! Yes! This my baby, right here. He belongs to me. This my little boy. Period!" She hollered, then got to bouncing up and down on me as if I was a bouncy house.

Simone put both of her thick thighs over my face and lowered herself enough for me to eat that pussy. That's exactly what I did.

By this time, her pussy was super salty and wet. I could hear her and Mrs. Jones kissing above me, and that kind of threw me for a loop at first. I didn't know if they were doing it for my benefit, or it was how they really got down behind closed doors. I mean, we were in Houston. In the south, that family with family shit was more normal than I think people really realized.

Mrs. Jones got to riding me so fast that it sounded like the headboard was about to go through the wall. I gripped her big ass and let her have me, slamming her down onto me, hard. There was nothing like having an older woman on top of you. A mother figure who knew how to get down. That shit was hot. Before she came, I was cumming deep in her womb and loving it, while Simone screamed and moaned on my attacking tongue. Then, she came, followed by her mother.

Afterwards, we laid in my bed with them rubbing all over my stomach and playing with my dick. I would take turns kissing one and then the other.

Mrs Jones broke the silence. "Shemar, I'm serious about what I said. I don't want to lose you when you turn eighteen. I'll do anything to keep you happy and safe with me, baby. You're my baby boy, and I love you. I'm going to help you get Purity so we can all be a family, if you'll allow me to." She sucked on my neck, and licked up the sweat from my chest.

Simone, not to be outdone, ran her tongue into my ear, and squeezed my dick before stroking it. "Long as I can have this right here, big bruh, I'll do anything. I belong to you, just like momma do. I gave you my virginity."

"Yeah, honey, and I gave her permission to. So what's it gon' be?" Mrs. Jones asked, sitting up enough to look into my face. Her titties wobbled on her chest. She smelled like sweat and sex. I loved it.

"Momma, if you gon' help me get her back, then I'll do whatever you want me to do. I don't want to leave y'all either. I feel like a King here." I was being honest. Where else could I go where a mother and daughter would be ready to get in the same bed with me. Both was thick as hell, and fine as a muthafucka. Freaks and heathens, just like me.

"I'm going to do everything in my power to take custody of her, starting tomorrow. I would have been did this, but Vincent was against it for whatever reason." She shook her head.

Simone sucked her teeth. "Yeah, but he got a whole other ass family that he don't think nobody knows about, and a twenty year old girl pregnant."

She rolled her eyes. "Mom, when are you going to leave him?"

Mrs. Jones was quiet for a long time, then she smiled, though her eyes seemed to be way off in the distance. "Soon, baby. Soon. Trust and believe that."

Chapter 11

The next day, as I was coming out of the Pastor's house, a money green Lexus pulled up on me, sitting on some thirty-inch gold rims. The windows were tinted black, and I could hear the sounds of "Money Bags Yo" beating from the speakers. I didn't know who the fuck it was, so I put my hand into the small of my back and gripped the handle of my .45. I was ready to start bussing, especially when the window rolled down slowly. I took a step back and pulled my pistol out and aimed that bitch right at the car.

"Shemar, chill out, nigga!" a familiar voice said. The window rolled all the way down and I saw that it was Chelsey sitting in the passenger's seat. "I got Nikki cousin with me. He down here from Brooklyn. and he wanna know what happened to her. I got my theories. but I felt that you could shed more light on the situation for him," she said, moving her head all funny; I guessed to get out of the scope of where I had my pistol aimed.

I kept it aimed at the car for a minute before I lowered it. My mind was fucked up because I could have sworn I'd told Nikki to smoke Chelsey's ass. Second to that, I knew that Nikki had a cousin that was out in Brooklyn by the name of Nut. She talked about him every now and then. I wondered if this was him, though she hadn't pulled my coat about nobody coming to Houston to visit.

I kept the pistol on the side of me and walked down the stairs. I didn't know if it was a set up or what, but in that moment, I really didn't care. I felt like whatever was gon' happen was gon' happen. It was nine in the morning, and it already looked like it was getting ready to rain. The air was thick with moisture.

I got to the car and Chelsey moved her big head backward so I could see who was behind the steering wheel. It was big, black, dark skinned nigga with waves in his hair. He had a scar on the right side of his face. He nodded to me and I nodded back.

Then, he opened his car door and got out, walking around the hood of it until he was standing about an arm's length away from me. "Yo', whut up, Sun? My name Nut. You that nigga Shemar, right?" he asked, curling his upper lip almost into a mug.

I tightened my grip on my pistol. "Yeah, that's me. You Nikki cousin?"

He nodded. "I was coming down here to surprise her ass, then when I touched down, I got to calling her back to back with no response. Finally, I reached out to Chelsey, and she tell me that my cousin been hit up. I wanna know what happened. I know she fuck with you on a daily basis, so you gotta know somethin'."

I looked this nigga up and down and got a lil' irritated because it sounded like he was trying to make it seem like I had something to do with my right hand getting hit up. I was ready to pop his ass and finish off Chelsey, if that's where he was going with things. I was already feeling some type of way about Chelsey being alive.

"Some niggas shot up her trap, and she wound up getting hit in the process. In the back and in the shoulder. Last time I checked on her in the hospital, she was on life support, and they had to revive her again. That's my heart right there, and these niggas ain't finna get away with that."

He scrunched his face. "You damn right, they ain't. We can go holler at whoever did it right now. Word is bond. The streets finna bleed over my lil' cousin, Kid. Who is these niggas?"

Chelsey stuck her head half way out of the window. "I know it had to be Bryan people because who else could've done something like that? He was working for Moncho and them, and when y'all got up with his glamour y'all took they money and dope in the process. That shit wasn't even his."

Now, I really wanted to blast this broad, because she was saying too much. Wasn't nobody supposed to know about that lick that we had pulled on her baby daddy, other than her and us. She was making it seem like some shit had been leaked to other sources.

I mugged the shit out of her with hatred. "What the fuck is you talking about, Chelsey? How would anybody else know about that lick?" I asked, walking to the passenger's window.

She sat back in her seat and started to bite on her bottom lip.

I stuck my head in the window, nearly bumped foreheads with her. She looked off into the distance and refused to make eye contact with me until I grabbed a handful I of her hair and gripped it hard. I wasn't a big fan of fucking over a woman, but when it came down to Nikki and those that I truly loved, I would body anybody. Period.

She screamed, and tried to yank her head away from me, but I held on.

"Tell me what's good, and I ain't play in either." I pulled her hair a lil' harder.

"Okay, okay, damn! Before y'all hit Bryan's punk ass, me and him got into it while his guy was over there. I was asking him about some money to take our child shopping, and he was trying to front on me in front of dude. Long story short, he was saying that he wasn't gon' give me shit, and that the next time I would get some money out of his ass that it would be during child support. Just so happens that I was on the phone with Nikki while I was arguing with his ass, and she asked me if that nigga got plenty paper in the house. I told her yeah. Then, she was like don't even trip, we gon' get more than child support out of his ass. I started laughing, and the nigga snatched the phone from me, and they got into an argument. I don't know what she was saying, but I heard him say, 'Bitch, if you ever think about hitting my trap, I'ma body yo' ass. Now try me.' Then, he hung my phone up and his guy got to asking him who she was, and all this other shit. The next night, y'all hit him, and his guy remembered those events, because he woke me up early in the morning, the next day after Bryan got stanked, along with that bitch, on some Gorilla shit."

Nut stomped over to the window and damn near pulled me out of it. He reached into it and grabbed her by the neck, choking her.

"Bitch, why you ain't tell me all of this shit last night? Fuckin' with you and that bum ass nigga, my lil' cousin done got hit up. I should stank yo' ass right here." He growled and forced her more deeply into the head rest.

I could hear her choking, as I took a step back and looked around to make sure that nobody was looking. I didn't give a fuck what he did to her. I was hoping he bodied her. I would even show him where we could get rid of the corpse.

She kicked her legs in the seat while I continued to act as a look out.

"Bitch, give me that nigga address, and where some of they other niggas stay at; whoever he was working for. Put that shit in my phone, right now!" He pushed her backward real hard, then dropped his phone in her lap.

Chelsey wrapped her hands around her neck and coughed for a few seconds. "I'm sorry, Nut, I didn't think to tell you or him. Please don't kill me. I'm begging you." She whimpered.

He reached into the window, picked up the phone and slammed it into her chest loudly. "Put the info in there and shut yo' ass up." I could tell that he was heated and a little crazy. It was the kind of nigga that I needed around me while I found out who did what to my heart, Nikki.

The rain started to come down harder. I watched Chelsey type a bunch of stuff into his phone. Then, she handed it to him. "That's Mickey info to where he live, and his number. I also gave you Sherm information because that's who he was selling for. So, if anybody came at Nikki, it was one of them. I know that for a fact." She looked like she was about to panic. "Now, can you just drop me off at home? I swear, I'm sorry."

Nut turned to me. "Look, Sun, I know my way around this bitch a lil' bit, but I need you to fuck with me and get at these niggas' heads in honor of my lil' cousin. I can't take this shit laying down, Shemar, and she already told me how you get down. So, what's the biz, Kid?"

I looked over my shoulder at the Pastor's house, because I could have sworn that I heard one of the windows opening. Sure as shit, I could see one of the curtains on the front window pulled to the side a bit. I guessed that it had to be either Mrs. Jones or Simone peeking out at me, but I didn't give a fuck. I was finna ride with the homie and get at them niggas' heads in honor of Nikki. I knew, without a shadow of a doubt, that she would blast for me, so I was finna blast for her.

I turned back to Nut. "Nigga, I'm with you. I got hella tools too if you ain't come equipped."

He curled his upper lip and nodded. "The Kid definitely need a few of them joints so we can set some shit off. Word is bond."

I told him to wait for me while I went and got what we needed, then he walked around to the driver's side and got in while Chelsey tried to explain herself to him.

I made my way to the basement and loaded up a duffle bag with two Mach .90's, with two eighty round clips apiece. Then, I snatched another .45 for me, and two for him, with three clips apiece that held ten shots. If I had my way, I would be using every bullet that I packed in honor if Nikki.

When I got to the top of the basement stairs, Mrs. Jones was waiting for me with a sad look on her face. I was about to shoot right past her because I didn't have time for that emotional shit right then. I needed for my heart to be cold, not warmed by her, so I thought about ignoring her, but I just couldn't, because I cared about her.

I got to the top of the stairs where she was standing, dropped the bag, and pulled her into me for a hug. "What's the matter, momma?"

She shook her head in the crook of my neck. "I know what you finna go out there and do, son, and I know I can't stop you. I'm just worried that something might happen to you. I don't know how I would take that. You're my baby boy. You're my absolute everything." She whimpered and cried into my neck. I could feel her tears wetting me.

I didn't want to get into all of that. I had to do what I had to do, and I wasn't about to let her stop me. I took a step back and held her in front of me at arm's length. "Look, momma, I gotta handle my business. Nikki is my heart, and I ain't finna let nobody violate her in any way without me standing up for her. You just gotta trust that I know what I'm doing, and you gotta hold me down like you supposed to, because this is who I am. You can't love me for who you want me to be, you have to love me for who I am. You understand that?" I rubbed her chin with my thumb.

She nodded and blinked tears that ran down her cheeks. "Yes, baby. Just be careful and know that momma is going to be right here, waiting on you. I need you just to be alive. Please, never forget that." She stepped forward and kissed me on the lips, then wrapped her arms around my neck.

I held her for what had to be two minutes, then broke our embrace. Afterward, I opened the back door and jogged around the house, jumping into the back of Nut's Lexus.

Chelsey was still in the front seat, apologizing. "I swear, y'all, I didn't know. Please, forgive me, and know that I would never do anything to hurt Nikki," she cried and sniffed snot back into her nose.

I didn't feel like hearing all that whining and shit because it wasn't gon' save Nikki. I texted Mrs. Jones and told her to make sure that she went and checked in on Nikki, and handled her business in regards to the custody placement of Purity. She responded by saying that she would be on top of it all day, and that gave me reassurance.

Nut was driving for about ten minutes when I noticed him pulling into an alley behind some seedy row houses on Center Drive. He drove about half way down the alley just as the rain started to beat against the car like crazy, then he stopped, and grabbed Chelsey by the neck, opening his driver's door while she kicked and screamed.

"No! No! Please, Nut! Please! Don't do this! I'm begging you!" She hollered, kicking and clawing at him.

He yanked her out of the car, and with two hands slammed her back against a burgundy rundown garage that had a stripped down car inside of it, sitting on bricks. He wrapped his hands around her neck and started to choke her. "Punk bitch. It's yo' fault. I always told her that fuckin' with you would be her down fall."

Chelsey hit at his arms as lightning flashed across the sky, and then thunder roared loudly. "Ack! Ack! I can't! Please!"

She tried kicking her legs at a useless attempt to break away. Had it been another day, I would have never watched a nigga choke a female out like he was doing, but due to the fact that I felt like she did have a hand in how Nikki got shot up, I didn't feel nothing. I got to looking at a few pics of me and my heart on my phone while Nut did his thing to her. The rain came down two times harder. It was damn near a wash-out.

Nut punched her in the stomach real hard, then choked her some more until her body went limp. He choked her for a little while longer, then lifted her into the air and threw her into the big, blue metal garbage can on the side of the garage, closing the top after he was done. He got back into the car, and I climbed over the seats until I was sitting in the passenger's.

"You good now, homie? You ready to go sweat this Mickey nigga?" I asked handing him a .45.

He wiped the water away from his fat face, then nodded. "Yeah, Kid. Let's make these bitch niggas feel that heat."

Ghost

Chapter 12

I really didn't know that nigga Mickey like that. I'd seen him a few times in Cloverland, but we had never exchanged any words. I was a lil' angry at Nikki for not telling me about the conversation with Bryan, prior to us hitting his ass, because I would have never allowed for us to hit that lick. Especially if his boy wasn't there for us to body as well as him. That left too many loose ends. All the while I was worried about Chelsey, I was missing a whole other ass person. Also, don't get it twisted, I still had that nigga Vito on my mind. I most definitely was gon' holler at him with Nut. I just wanted to handle one thing at a time, that way we didn't move sloppy or miss nothing.

An hour after Nut bodied Chelsey, we parked a block away from Mickey's baby's mother's house. I guess when I was in the crib, talking to Mrs. Jones, Chelsey had told Nut that Mickey was always at his baby mother's crib, out in The Heights. We rolled down the street where her duplex was and saw a candy painted purple Benz parked in front of the house. That automatically made me think that it had to be him, even though I didn't know what kind of whip he drove. To make things simpler, his license plates read "Mickey". So, we parked a block over and loaded up with the .45s.

"Yo, Sun, you sure Kid ain't ever seen you before?" Nut asked, cocking back one of the guns.

I took my ski mask out of my duffle and slid it over my face. "N'all. I ain't ever fucked with them niggas like that. I don't trust niggas. Only person I jam with in the game is Nikki. Been like that ever since we jumped off the porch."

He nodded. "Word. That's what's up, Dunn." He took a ski mask out of the crack of his driver's seat and slid it down his face. "Let's go, Sun."

We jumped out of the whip and into the pouring rain, jogging down the alley until we came to a house that was directly across the street from Mickey's BM's place. Once there, we crouched down and I peeped out the scene. The street looked deserted, and I imagined it was because it was raining so hard, and it was windy as hell. I was drenched and hadn't been out of the car for five minutes yet. I was hoping Houston wasn't finna undergo another hurricane. Our city couldn't sustain that shit already.

Atfter feeling like the coast was going to be clear for a little while, I got antsy, even though I didn't know how we were about to get into this house. "Say, Nut, how we finna get in this muhfucka? What? We finna just kick the doe in or somethin'?" I asked, trying to see what his game plan was.

"Nah, Kid. Chelsey say they sell weed out her crib. I'ma just knock on the doe, and once Blood open it, we gon' bum rush his ass. Simple as that. Brooklyn style, baby."

I had never been to Brooklyn before, so I didn't know how they got down out there. But I was from Houston, bred by the slums through and through, and if ever I sold anything out of a house, I was strapped at all times. Especially when I answered the door. So, I had to imagine that Mickey would be too. I wasn't cool with this plan. I felt that it was a reckless one, and I was smarter than that.

"N'all, that shit ain't gon' work. We gon' fuck with this nigga whip, make that alarm go off, then when he open that door, we gon' bum rush his ass. He might still have that pistol with him, but his eyes gon' be on his whip, and we gon' already be on the porch; you feel me?"

He pulled his mask down a little further. "Say, Kid, it's yo' city; I'ma follow you. I just wanna snuff this nigga for Nikki's sake."

Thunder roared overhead, and lightning flashed across the sky as me and Nut ran across the street onto the side of Mickey's BM's crib. Then, we climbed up the banister and waited on the side of the door. I took the medium sized rock that I had picked up and threw it at Mickey's whip with all of my might. *Peck!* It crashed against the paint but the alarm didn't go off.

"Fuck!" I said, then hopped off of the porch in search for another one.

I could barely see in front of me as I looked along the side of the house for another rock. I could hear music coming from inside of the house. I swept my foot along the side of the duplex, hoping to discover another rock to throw at his whip. I got irritated when I didn't see one. I walked along the back of the house in search of one, and got into the backyard when I heard Nut's voice.

"Bitch ass niggas, put y'all hands up right the fuck now! Hurry up!" he hollered.

I almost broke my neck when turning around and running alongside the gangway, until I got back to the porch, where I hopped over the banister and saw that Nut had his .45 with the barrel pressed under Mickey's chin.

In Mickey's arms was a little boy. Behind him was a light skinned female with way too much make up on. I assumed she was his baby's mother. She threw her arms all the way up in the air. On the side of her was a dark-skinned nigga with nasty red eyes. He looked almost sickly. He scrunched his face and looked like he had something up his sleeve before I upped my .45 and barged into the door, pressing my gun to his cheek.

"Nigga, who else in here?" I asked through clenched teeth.

He closed his eyes but the mug on his face didn't change. "Man, we the only ones here. What the fuck dis about, my nigga?"

The female started to whimper right away. "Please, don't hurt my baby. Please, I'll do anything. I got the combination to his safe. It's in my hall linen closet. I'll give you everything. Just don't hurt my lil' boy." She cried and tried to pull him out of Mickey's arms.

Mickey scrunched his face. "Tina, shut yo' ass up, damn!" He pulled the little boy out of her grasp.

Nut grabbed him by the neck and poked him in the cheek with his pistol. "Nigga, you shut yo' bitch ass up. Tina, we gon' need all that that paper, and if you cooperate, we'll let you and that lil' boy go, but these niggas in jeopardy." He kicked the door closed behind him. "Nigga, give her the baby before I splash yo' ass, right here."

Mickey handed the little boy over to Tina, and she wrapped him in her arms, lovingly.

"Look, man, y'all can have that paper. Just take that shit and go. I know when I'm caught off guard. It is what it is," Mickey said with his head leaned all the way to the left because of Nut's pistol.

I grabbed the other nigga by his neck and put the .45 to his forehead, before slamming him up against the wall. "Nigga, open yo' mouth," I demanded through clenched teeth.

He looked at me like I was crazy.

"Fuck that, playboy, this goin' in a sheet." Then, I looked to Tina. "This nigga Mickey yo' only source of income to take care of yo' son?" I asked her while putting all of the stuff out of the safe into a white sheet.

She shook her head. "N'all, I work. He barely help me with my son. He just as trifling as all the rest of these men in Houston. He treat me like a baby momma, and my son is his seventh child."

I was amazed that during all of this shit, she still had enough guts to give me a glance into their relationship. I hated worthless niggas all around the board.

I grabbed a stack of the money and gave it to her. It had to be about ten gees. I felt like she deserved it because we were finna body her baby daddy. "Look, shawty, I'm gon' let you live, but I don't want you to play me. Take this money, and you and yo' son go out that back doe and keep running. We got niggas outside the house that's gon' be watching you, so don't try and get no help, or they gone body y'all ass. Just think about yo' son and yo' life. Fuck that nigga Mickey. You hear me, Goddess?"

She took the money and nodded. "Yes, I do, and I thank you so much. I know you could kill me but thank you." She started crying.

I got up and led her to the back door and opened it. "Look, my niggas out there, so just keep running, and get away from here. Save yo' lil' man. Mickey sins done caught up with him. Now, go!" I pushed her slightly into the rain and watched her take off through the backyard with her arms wrapped around her son, and the money still in her hand.

I couldn't kill that woman, man. Neither her nor her son deserved to die, but since I had let her go, I knew that me and Nut had to hurry up. I closed the door, grabbed our money and dope, and met him in the living room.

He stood over Mickey with the hammer to his pistol cocked back. "Bitch ass nigga, which one of you muhfuckas shot up my lil' cousin house the other night? I ain't gon' ask y'all again." He stepped on to Mickey's chest with one foot.

The other nigga sat with his back against the wall, bleeding profusely from his mouth. I guessed that when I went to the back to handle business with Tina, Nut got busy on his ass because he was fucked up, breathing all heavy and everything.

Mickey shook his head. "Bruh, I ain't shoot up nobody crib. I don't even know who yo' lil' cousin is. I was here all day, bagging up my work for the last two days. You can ask Tina, and she'll tell you the same thing."

Nut stomped him in the ribs. "Fuck nigga, you lying. That bitch Chelsey already fingered you. She said you was over there when her and Bryan was arguing about some money, then she got on the phone with my lil' cousin, before that nigga grabbed the phone from her on some gangsta shit, and got to talking about what my lil' cousin should and shouldn't do. Fuck nigga, keep that shit one hundred."

"Nigga, who is yo' cousin? You steady saying cousin like we supposed to know who he is, and we can't even see yo' face. Who is he, homie?" the other nigga asked, then coughed up a loogey of blood. He tried to spit, but it was so thick that it got caught on his chin and hung there.

I was tired of his mouth, and I knew we was on the clock. I knelt and turned my pistol around, exposing the metal handle, took it and slammed it into his forehead with all of my might. *Bam!*

"I'm tide of this nigga slick mouth. We gotta get the fuck out of here," I said as I watched blood ooze out of the hole in his head.

"Uhh. Uhh. What the fuck, man? I'm just trying to see who he is. I know I ain't shot up nobody crib. Y'all got the wrong one." He put his hand up to his wound and I watched blood seep out of the cracks of his fingers.

I ain't feel shit for him. I was ready to get out of there. "Man, fuck this nigga, big homie." I turned the gun around, aimed for his face and pulled the trigger in honor of Nikki. *Boom! Boom!*

The bullets slammed into his cheek twice, and turned his neck all the way to the right while his blood splattered against the wall like tomato paste. I could smell the gun powder mixed with the scent of copper. He slumped forward with his eyes wide open. My gun smoked from the barrel.

Mickey started to shake his head. "Look, that shit between Nikki and Bryan. It ain't have nothin to do with me. If anything, you gotta holler at that nigga Sherm!" He jumped up and crashed against Nut.

Nut almost tackled him into the wall, then Mickey made his way toward the front of the house. Nut fell backward, and bussed in the air, sending a bullet to the upstairs neighbors. I aimed my gun and bussed at Mickey twice. *Boom! Boom!* I watched a bullet slam into his shoulder.

"Arrgh! You muthafucka!" he hollered, before jumping through the front room window.

By this time, Nut gathered himself, and we ran to the front of the house and looked out of the window in time to see Mickey running across the street at full speed, holding his shoulder. He looked like he was about to fall over.

I could hear police sirens in the distance. I let them hammers slam. *Boom! Boom! Boom! Boom! Boom! Boom! Boom!*

He twisted around in the street, fell, and then got back up and took off running along the side of somebody's house until he disappeared.

I was out of my mind with panic. The sirens got closer, and Mickey was nowhere to be seen. "Come on, Nut, let's get the fuck out of here, nigga." I grabbed the sheet with all of the shit in it.

We hit the back door, running full speed until we got to the alley, where we jumped one of the neighbors' fences, wound up in their backyard as the rain came down so hard that I couldn't see shit really.

I almost bussed my shit more than once, and due to the fact that Nut was a big nigga, he was having a hard time keeping up with me.

I made it to his car first, and a minute later, he showed up wheezing like he was about to have an asthma attack. As soon as he got to the car, we loaded up and stormed away from there. I couldn't believe that we had fucked off the way that we did.

Ghost

Chapter 13

We wound up at the Super 8 Motel where Nut was staying. I paced the floor for a whole hour, while he laid on his back on the bed, looking like he was about to die. "Nigga we fucked up. We let that nigga live. We fucked up, bruh. We gotta figure this shit out," I said, feeling like I was about to have a nervous breakdown.

I didn't know who was gon' come at us first. Was it gon' be the police, or was it gon' be that nigga Sherm after Mickey told him everything that happened. I didn't know if they knew who I was, but me and Nikki was always together. It was damn near impossible to find her without me. Then, it wasn't no telling how much Chelsey ran her mouth; not mention her murder. It was so much shit to worry about that I started to get sick. I didn't know what to do.

"We gotta find out what hospital dude in and finish the job. That's if he even made it."

He sat up on the bed and took a deep breath, exhaling slowly through his nose. I could hear him wheezing a lil' bit. "We was off Park Avenue, right? So, what's the closest hospital they a take Sun to from there?" he asked, before reaching into his pocket and pulling out a gray inhaler. He shook it up and down, and then sucked the mist into his lungs loudly.

I shook my head. "We ain't getting in no hospital with guns in Houston. They police presence is crazy now. Our best bet is to keep our ears to the street to try and find out if that nigga survived them shells. If he did, we gotta find out what state he in. Hopefully, he bled out on the next block or somethin'." I mean it was the best I could come up with right then, because there was so much shit going through my mind.

"Yo, no matter what, we gotta get at that Sherm nigga. The way they was talking, that nigga Sherm definitely had something to do with my lil' cousin getting hit up," Nut said, shaking his inhaler again and sucking the mist into his lungs. He closed his eyes and I noticed his chest got real big before he exhaled slowly.

I nodded. "I agree, but let's just lay low for a few days, and then we'll see what our next move should be. This where you gon' be at?" I asked, grabbing my half of the merch, ready to hit the door. I had already called Mrs. Jones to pick me up around the corner. I needed to get away from the homie for a while so I could collect my thoughts. Plus, I was missing Nikki. I was gon' have Mrs. Jones swing me by the hospital so I could put my lips to her skin. I felt like I needed to just touch her to restore my soul.

Nut nodded. "Yeah, Kid. I might hit up a strip club or somethin' later, but for now I'ma take a nap and rest my lungs. Give me yo' number and shit so I can get up with you tomorrow or somethin'."

I did just that before I left his room and met up with Mrs. Jones.

After we swung by the crib and I put the rest of that shit into my storage, she drove me to the hospital so I could see Nikki. By the grace of God, she was doing a little better. Though they still had her in the intensive care unit, she was no longer on life support.

She was breathing on her own and had already received a blood transfusion. I wasn't her blood type, and had I been, I would have given her every drop of blood inside of my body, along with my heart. The longer she stayed in that hospital, the more I discovered how much I really loved my right hand woman.

I stepped into her room and felt my throat get tight right away. She was laying in the bed on her side, with her eyes closed. She was still hooked up to a few machines, but not as many as before. I thanked God for that.

I walked over to her, kneeled and kissed her on the cheek, before laying my face sideways on to hers. She smelled like the hospital. I was used to her smelling like Prada or Burberry perfume. It was just another reminder of what we were going through. I was realizing all of the small things that I cherished about her, that I had not noticed before. I moved her hair away from her face and kissed her on her small forehead, then rubbed that spot with my thumb. Her eyes flickered but did not open.

I laid my face back onto hers. "I love you so much, Nikki, and I miss you just as much. I hate that you gotta go through this, but I know you gon' pull through. They ain't hollering that life support crap no more. Now they saying that you're slowly recovering, but I already knew that you would be. We always said that we was gon' go see our Maker together. When you go, I go. That's the way it gotta be. You're my heart. If you stop, then I die, and vice versa. Our loyalty is in blood. Always have been."

I kept my face against hers for about two minutes without saying a word. I could hear the machines beeping, and people walking back and forth in the hallway. I knew I couldn't stay there for long, but I didn't want to leave her again. I wished that she could wake up and wrap her little arms around me, or cuss me out or something. I missed her voice, her attitude, her hugs.

Mrs. Jones came over and rubbed me on the back. "Shemar, I think we should get out of here because it's been a detective coming around, asking questions about her. I don't want you getting caught up in no drama right now. I need you, Simone needs you, Purity needs you, and most of Nikki is going to need you when she wakes up."

I kept my face on Nikki's for a short while longer, then pulled back, just looking her over. She had lost weight and her skin was a little dry, but she was still more beautiful than ever. I kissed each of her eye lids, and then her lips. Afterward, I laid my head on her chest and listened to her heartbeat. I missed her like crazy. I put my lips to her ear. "Nikki, I'm killing these niggas one at a time until I find out who did this to you. I love you, girl. You are my everything. I pledge my loyalty to you until they take the air out of my lungs."

The car ride home was real quiet for half the way there, until Mrs. Jones reached over and squeezed my hand. "Baby, she gon' be okay. You have to know that. I need you to focus some on helping me get Purity out of the Deacon's care. I should be able to have a sit down with him and his wife this Sunday after church. They have already agreed to it. Now all

I have to do is get Vincent on board, but you know how stubborn your father is." She rolled her eyes and brought the car to a halt as she pulled up to the red light.

"Momma, don't call dude that. He ain't my pops. My old man been dead for a little while now."

She nodded and made a sympathetic face. "I know, baby, but you know what I mean."

I did, but I still ain't like dude being referred to as my father. Like I said before, I ain't have nothing against the Pastor. I just really didn't like men to begin with. I didn't know why I was like I was.

"Well, I'ma need you to get him on board, 'cause my little sister gotta come from over there. I'm tired of going to sleep at night and not knowing if she's safe and sound. The Deacon has a house full of predators, and that's including him. I swear if one of them hurt my lil' sister, I'ma run through that whole house with murder on my mind." I could already imagine it, and it was making my heart beat faster and faster.

Mrs. Jones pulled off into traffic. "Well, I'll do everything that I possibly can, so you don't worry about it. All I ask is that you stay out of trouble so that it makes things easier. Can you promise me that?"

I let my seat back a lil' bit and closed my eyes. "Momma, I can't make that promise because it's so much going on already." I didn't know how much more trouble I was gon' get into before she even had the first sit down with the Deacon and his wife. Apart of me felt like I was living on borrowed time, and I didn't know what to do.

I must've been laying in my bed on my back with my eyes open for about three hours when the door opened, and Simone snuck into my room and got into the bed with me. She got under the covers and laid her head on my chest. "I been missing you a whole lot, Shemar, to the point that it's been driving me crazy. I think I'm becoming obsessed with you or something. What should I do?" she asked and kissed me on the naked chest.

I laid there for a minute, taking in what she had said, but still thinking about the event with me and Nut. Then, I got to thinking about Nikki and Purity. I knew that I needed to save the both of them, but it was driving me crazy trying to figure it all out. Now, *she* was acting like she really needed me.

"Simone, you just feeling that way because you gave me your virginity. After that happens, the next stage is going to be you clinging to me because at every turn, you'll wonder if I'll kick you to the curb now that I have everything that you can possibly offer me right now, that was most sacred to you. You're vulnerable. It's normal," I said, wrapping my arm around her protectively.

She rubbed up and down my abs. "So, are you going to kick me to the curb now that you got it? I mean, what comes next for the boy?" She looked up into my face, curious, and really vulnerable. I could also detect that she was a little scared of what I might say.

I put my hand to the side of her face and held it, smiling down at her; my hazel eyes looking into her brown ones. "You're safe with me, Simone. Your virginity was just as special to me, and I took it as a gift from an angel. You're my baby, and I got you." I leaned down and kissed her on the forehead, but she lifted her face all the way up until her lips were against mine.

She closed her eyes, and I kissed her for a long time, giving her what she needed. Then, she straddled me, and sat up, looking down on me while biting on her bottom lip. She looked sexy as hell; I had to admit that.

"Shemar, I wanna do it again. I wanna feel you inside of me, because ever since you pulled out of me, I been feeling empty. Can you just give me some real quick? I promise I ain't gon' make that much noise." She lowered her mound onto the front of my boxers and ground herself against me.

She was only wearing a short, silk gown. I didn't know until that moment that she had already removed her panties. I could feel her heat almost immediately.

"Simone, yo' daddy out there somewhere, and you know he gotta get up in a lil' while. If he catch you in my room, that fool gon' go ballistic. You already know that," I said, feeling my dick get harder and harder.

She had her eyes closed, humping into me, moaning already. Her pretty face was scrunched up and her lil' pussy was already dripping wet, soaking my boxers. She reached her hand between us and grabbed my dick. "But I need you, big bruh. I need you inside me again. Please? Ever since you put it all the way in me, I ain't been able to sleep. All I think about is you doing it to me again, real hard, like you did before." She somehow managed to get my piece out of my boxer's hole. She was stroking me up and down, then she pulled the skin all the way back on him and put the head on her sex lips, sliding him into her wet hole.

I ain't have no self-control, because as soon as I felt him slip past her lips, I grabbed her round booty and pulled the cheeks apart, while she slid down my pole until she was sitting on my balls.

"Unnn. You in me again, baby. Ummm, it feels so good, I swear." She moaned, rocking back and forth real slowly, while she squeezed my chest. "Unn! Unn! Unn! Shit! Unn-a! Unn-a! Yes, big bruh. Shit." She rode me faster now. Her head was tilted backward with her mouth wide open.

I pulled the gown up to her stomach so I could look down and watch how my dick went in and out of her pussy. Her thick brown lips sucked at my pipe every time she rocked backward. Then, when she humped forward, her lips opened all the way up and exposed some of her pink. Bubbles from her juices formed around my invading stalk, and her clit was sitting fat at the top of her lips. The whole scene drove me crazy. I grabbed her ass and made her fuck me faster, pulling the top of her gown down, exposing her pretty titties. I sucked on the nipples, nipping at them with my teeth.

She sped up the pace, and scrunched her face. "Unnn-A! Shemar! Uh! Uh! Uh! Ummm-hmm! Uh! Uh! Shit, big bruh. This dick so good."

I sucked at her big nipples and forced her to take all of my dick. Her tight lil' pussy was eating me too, and spitting juices all down my balls. When I felt her starting to shake, I gripped her ass and forced her to fuck me harder. She bit into my shoulder and screamed with it muffling it.

"Yeah, cum on big bruh, baby. Cum on this dick. It's okay. It's okay, baby. You safe." I bounced her down on me a few more time, then I was cumming deep within her womb while my abs contracted again and again.

She must've felt it because it brought on another orgasm from her. She bounced up and down on me. Her eyes rolled into the back of her head, before she came again. I rubbed all over that ass, running my finger along the crack, wanting to push it into her asshole.

"Shemar. Shemar. From the back, please. Please, fuck me from the back, then I'll go back to my room and I'll leave you alone for the rest of the day. I promise. Please, big bruh. I need it so bad." She whimpered, already climbing off of me and getting on all fours on my carpet in the room. She put her face to the floor and spread her ass cheeks wide, exposing her fat pussy and small lil' crinkled asshole.

I shook my head. Once again, I didn't have no self-control. I started to stroke my dick in my fist while getting down to the floor behind her. I took my head, put it on her lips and pushed in with force, feeling her heat surround me.

"Uhh! Shit! Ummm. Every time. Every time you get in me, I love it," she whimpered, and lowered her face back to the carpet.

I grabbed a handful of her hair and yanked her head back a lil' bit. "I'm finna show you how I'm supposed to hit this pussy." I reached and threw a pillow from the bed to her. "Bite on this and be quiet."

She grabbed the pillow and looked over her shoulder. "Fuck me hard, Shemar. Stop playin' with me. Fuck me like you be doing my momma. I'm ready now." She bit on the pillow and closed her eyes.

I gripped her hips and started to fuck her with all of my might. I mean I was killing that pussy like I hated it, but in reality it was so good that I was making some weird ass noises that I wasn't proud of. Her ass bounced back into me, wobbling and shaking while her hard nipples dragged across the carpet. I reached under her and gripped them, pulling on the nipples while she screamed into the pillow. I felt her cumming on me again, and that made me speed up the pace until I was cumming deep within her, again and again. I was having so much fun with that pussy that I didn't even know that the Pastor had opened the door and was watching us in action, and had been for about five minutes.

Chapter 14

Something told me to look over my shoulder, and when I did, I saw him standing in the doorway with his mouth wide open. He looked pissed. I pulled out of Simone and slapped her on the ass. She was still moaning into the pillow. I noticed that when I pulled out, she had her hand between her thick thighs, pinching her clitoris.

She looked back at me, irritated. "Bruh, why you Pullout? I was finna cum again. Please, just—" She must've looked up and saw her father, because the next thing I knew, she jumped up to her feet and pulled her gown down. "Daddy, I can explain. Me and Shemar was just. I mean. Well, I guess, I was just—"

He stepped forward and grabbed her by the neck, picking her up into the air. "You little fast ass bitch. How dare you bring that sin down on this family? That is your brother!" He slammed her against the wall and continued to choke her.

I jumped up and threw on my boxers, before going over and slapping at his hand. "Man, let her go. What the fuck is wrong with you Pastor?"
He backhanded me with his knuckles, and bussed my nose right away. I fell backward and down to one knee. I felt woozy and everything. I guessed because I had cum so much inside of Simone that I was literally weak.

Mrs. Jones ran in from the living room and attacked him. "You let her go, you son of a bitch! You're hurting her!" she screamed.

All he did was push her in the chest, then slammed Simone into the wall again, continuing to choke her.

"Ack! Ackkk! Dad! Let me go! I can't!" She kicked her legs and tried to swing at him. Her gown was coming up around her waist, exposing her nakedness underneath.

The Pastor frowned and then put two hands around her neck, really squeezing. "Die, little girl. You have disgraced this family. You are no longer pure. You are the whore of Babylon. Die! Ahhh!" He squeezed tighter.

By this time, I had got a hold of myself. I ran over to him and punched him with all of my might, right in the kidney. *Whom!* Then again in the back. *Bam!* "Let her go, and fight *me*, nigga."

He dropped her and fell against the wall. "Aww, you ungrateful son of a bitch!" He bounced up from one knee and rushed me with his guards to the side of his face.

As soon as he got close enough, he punched me straight in the mouth, and then followed with a right hook that knocked me down to one knee again. The Pastor was every bit of two hundred and fifty pounds, and back in the day, he had been a boxer and a gangsta. I didn't learn all of this until after this night.

"Leave him alone!" Simone jumped on his back and tried to choke him from the back. "You're just a big bully, dad. I love him!"

He grabbed her arms and slowly pulled them apart, then he flung her to the floor. "What! You love yo' own freaking brother!" He raised his foot as if he were going to stomp her in the stomach.

I tackled his bitch ass hard into the dresser. *Whoom!* His back hit it, and I jumped up and punched him right into his nose with all of my might. *Bam!* His head flew backward and hit the dresser, then he punched me in the nuts. I wanted to cry like a little girl that somebody had punched in the stomach. I fell to my knees, holding my nuts, and wound up on my side with tears running down my eyes. It felt like my nuts were in my stomach and my ass at the same time. I was sick.

"Lil' Boy! How dare you defy me and betray me in this manner? Don't you understand what all I went through for you!" He knelt at the side of me and smacked me on the face so hard that I saw blue lightning behind my eyes. I mean he hit me hard.

I rolled over onto my stomach and tried to breathe. My were nuts still killing me, and now my face.

He got up and grabbed Simone by the neck again. "You gotta die, you Jezebel. You will not bring Satan upon this household. Die! Die! Die!"

He must've been choking her super hard, because all I could hear were the steady sounds of *ack, ack, ack.* Her legs swung in the air as she tried to get him to drop her. He had her once again with her back against the wall.

I was trying to get a hold of my breathing because I couldn't breathe at all. My nuts felt like they were so far up in my stomach that I was about to throw up. I knew that I had to get to my feet to save Simone or he was going to kill her. So, I took a deep breath, exhaled and slowly got to my feet, then I ran over to him on wobbly legs, and elbowed him in the back of the head. Afterward, I wrapped my arm around his neck and fell to the ground with him, after he dropped Simone onto her back.

"Get off of me, boy! I done told you already. No weapons formed against me shall prosper!" He stood up with me on his back, then he ran backward and crashed my back into the dresser.

I held on tight, even though the corner of it had slammed into my side, causing me a great deal of pain. "Simone, y'all get out of here. Let me handle him!" I said, out of breath and unsure of myself. I didn't think I could fuck in the Pastor's business.

He was too strong, and he seemed like the angrier he got, the stronger he became. I was struggling already. I wanted to pop him and get it over with, but I knew that I couldn't do that. I couldn't kill nor shoot the man because that would jeopardize everything for Purity. I had to just accept this ass whooping on behalf of myself and Simone. I was careless. I knew better, and I had to face his fury.

He stood all the way up and flung me over his shoulder, onto my back, just as Simone was on her way out of the room. Before she could cross the threshold, he grabbed a handful of her hair and yanked her back into the room. I didn't know where Mrs. Jones was, but I was glad that she wasn't going through the abuse or experiencing his wrath.

"Ahhh! Let me go, Daddy! You're out of your freaking mind!" Simone screamed, before he picked her up and threw her against the wall, knocking her out immediately. She fell on her side, and rolled over onto her face, unmoving.

Then, he kneeled and wrapped his big ass hands around my neck. "You betrayed me, Shemar! You betrayed me like Absalom did David, and your sentence is death!" He got to choking me with all of his might while he straddled me and sat on my stomach.

When I tell you that the blow that he had given me to the nuts was affecting me like crazy, please believe me. I could not breathe. Every time I inhaled, I felt like I wanted to throw up. So, as he choked me, all I could do was just let him. I was too weak to do anything else.

"Die, son! Die, and Lord forgive me for taking you off of this earth." He squeezed his hands around my neck tighter and tighter.

By this time, my vision was going blurry. Things were becoming fuzzy and I was starting to make my peace with death. I was tired. I was ready to go, if it was meant for me to go this way. I looked into his blurry face and I saw the spit dripping from the corner of his mouth. His eyes were deranged and in a far off place. Murder had to be on his mind, and I made my peace with that. I simply quit fighting, feeling guilty for not being able to protect Nikki. Guilty for now having enough self-control to stay away from Simone, while her father was in the house. Guilty for not having a solid plan to save Purity from the sick ass Deacon and his sons. I felt like a failure. A loser, and a complete waste of space.

I felt all of my blood rush to my head, and then my lungs started to hurt as if I had been stabbed in them. My vision turned red. Just as I was about to fade out, I heard a loud ass *clunk, clunk, clunk!*

"Get yo' ass off of my son!" *Clunk! Clunk!*

The next thing I knew, the Pastor was falling off of me after his blood spurted across my face. I looked up to see Mrs. Jones standing over him with one of his golf clubs. She raised it over her head and brought it down again across his back. *Bam!*

"Awww! Vicki! What the hell are you doing?" he asked, with blood running out of the back of his head, onto his neck, before saturating his shirt. He crawled around on all fours.

Mrs. Jones sized him up real quick before slamming the driver of the club onto his back. "Hypocrite!" *Bam!* He jerked and fell onto his back with his arms covering his face. "You think I don't know that you have a whole other family outside of this one?" *Bam!*

"Aww! Baby, I'm sorry!" he hollered, curling up into a ball. *Bam!* "Awww!" he hollered as she attacked him again, this time hitting him in the stomach with it causing him to sit up, only to curl back into a protective ball.

She walked around him. "You sick son of a bitch! What kind of man preys on the women of his congregation? Then gets one pregnant that he knew ever since she was born into this world? For God's sake, we used to babysit Felicia!" *Bam!* She brought the club down again, this time connecting with the Pastor's arms. I could hear it crash against his bones.

Than must've been all that he could take because he rolled his big ass under the bed, out of the way of her assaults. "Vicki, this ain't about me. It's about our children, in our home, screwing each other. Why are you making this about me?" he hollered.

I tried my best to get up, holding my stomach. I kneeled beside Simone to see if she was okay, tapping her on the cheek until her eyes opened. Then, I helped her up and wrapped one of her arms around my neck. "Come on, sis, let's get you out of here," I said, making our way to the door while Mrs. Jones got to her knees and got to poking him with the golf club.

"Because, it is about you. How dare you crucify these children for their sins, when yours are two times greater? You have a child out of wedlock by a girl that we used to care for. Then, you have a whole other family by a woman that we went to college with. A woman who smiles in my face every Sunday as if I don't know what's going on between you two. I know about your two sons with her. I know that you don't let them come to the services because they look too much like you. You are a hypocrite, Vincent! Now, get from under there!" she screamed, poking at him again.

"Oww! Oww! Would you stop it, woman! Give me this gotdamn club!" He yanked it out of her hand.

This made Mrs. Jones stand straight up and run out of the room, bumping me and Simone on her way past. She disappeared down the hallway, into their bedroom, as the Pastor climbed from under the bed.

I was worried that he was going to try and attack Simone again, so I placed her behind me protectively and sized him up. "Look, Pastor, leave her alone, man. She's just a kid and you a grown man. You shouldn't be putting your hands on her, and sho' not around her neck. Just let this stuff go," I said, feeling sick on the stomach.

He looked as if he was about to attack us, but then his eyes got as big as paper plates as he looked over my shoulder.

Mrs. Jones pushed me and Simone out of the way, holding a big ass .357 in her two hands with the hammer already cocked back. "That's okay, Shemar, I'm gon' put an end to this, right away. I'm tired of this son of a bitch. You attacked my daughter, my son, then me. You cheated and broke our home apart, way before any of us indulged in any sin in this house. Now you die!" She aimed the gun at his head, ready to pull the trigger, I imagined.

The Pastor threw his hands in the sky. "Please, don't, Vicki. I'm sorry, baby. I'll leave. I'll give you this house. Just please don't kill me. I'm sorry for putting my hands on you all. It's just that seeing them together was too much for me. As far as everything else you said, well, I—"

"I don't care! Just get the fuck out of here, Vincent, and never return. Go! Live with your other family and be happy, because we are. We don't need you. You are the main hypocrite here, and it would be better if you weren't around." She lowered her eyes into slits. "So, what's it gon' be?"

He stared at her for a long time. "So, you gon' choose them over me? After all that we've been through?" He looked hurt.

She curled her upper lip. "In a heartbeat. Hit the road, Jack."

The Pastor moved his things out of the house the next morning in silence. As crazy as it may sound, I helped him move, even though we didn't say a word to each other. The night before, I held Simone while she cried against me, and we listened to Mrs. Jones and the Pastor talk about how they were going to split up the assets between one another. I think that Simone was sick that her parents were splitting up, but even more so that she was the cause of it. I tried my best to reassure her that it was for the better, and that now with him gone, me and her could enjoy each other whenever we wanted to, because Mrs. Jones wasn't tripping about us getting down together, and that was half the battle. That made her smile.

After the Pastor's U-Haul truck was loaded up as much as it could be, he looked toward the house and shook his head. "This ain't over, Shemar. Trust me when I tell you that I will never accept this." Then, he got into the truck and slammed the door before starting it and pulling off down the road.

I watched the truck for a long time until it disappeared. I didn't know what he meant by that, so I didn't want to let it bother me too much. Looking back, I wished that I would have.

After he left, and Simone went to school, I walked into Mrs. Jones bedroom and saw that she was sitting on the edge of the bed in her gown, with tears running down her cheeks. So, I slid beside her and put my left arm around her. "It's okay, momma. I swear, I got you. I know that you did all of this for me, and I won't take it for granted. Yo' son gon' hold you down. I promise." I kissed her on the side of the lips, before turning her face all the way to me so I could attack her thick lips a lot better. Then I licked her tears from her cheeks.

I knew that I had to go overboard and really make a statement, because she was feeling some type of way about everything, and I didn't want her to break down and drown deep within her emotions. I needed for her to know that I was there for her, and always would be.

She smiled weakly after I licked her tears from her face. Then, she grabbed both of my hands and looked into my eyes. "Shemar, I would do anything for you. I love you, and you're my son. You drive me so crazy, baby, and I have never been complete, until I adopted you as my son. Every woman needs a son like you to make them feel whole, because the men of this world are so trifling." She blinked, and a few tears sailed down her cheeks. "As soon as a hint of gravity shows up on the body, or a few years pass away and a man catches the eye of a younger woman, we are kicked to the curb. He no longer desires us in the way that he used too, and it hurts so bad, baby. It hurts so, so bad." She whimpered before laying her head on my shoulder.

I kissed her cheek and pulled her closer to me. "Momma, I will always love and desire you. You're the most beautiful woman in this world to me, and I belong to you. Always have, always will. Whenever you need me to heal you, just say so, and I will be there for you. I promise."

This made her cry harder. She wrapped her arms around me and cried into my armpit, pulling on my shirt. I could tell that she was in some serious emotional pain. "Shemar, never call me Mrs. Jones again, baby. Please. I am your mother. I belong to you, son. I no longer belong to that man. He's not worthy of me or anybody in this family. I mean that."

I held her for a few more moments, then pulled her all the way up along the bed until our backs were up against the headboard. Then, I just held her. "No more of that Mrs. Jones crap, momma. From now on, you're just my mother. How does that sound?"

She squeezed me tighter and cried harder into my chest. "Perfect, baby. Just like you. It sounds perfect."

Ghost

Chapter 15

Nut texted me later, at like two in the morning, saying that it was urgent and that he needed me to meet him at his room. So, after explaining to my mother that I had to go out and handle some business, I slipped out of the crib, and met up with him at the Super 8.

When I came through the door, the first thing I noticed was that he had guns all over the bed, and that fool Tim was also sitting next to the nightstand, smoking on a blunt. I didn't like the sight of that already because I felt like our backs were against the wall with the law and a few of the niggas out of Cloverland. I knew that Tim was a young nigga and often ran his mouth too much. I wanted to know why Nut had chosen to snatch lil' homie up.

Nut closed the door behind me and locked it, then walked over to Tim and grabbed the blunt from him. "This nigga say he know where that nigga Sherm stay, and that he can get us through the door because Sherm got him selling that dog food for him. So, I wanna hit that nigga before I go back to Brooklyn."

Tim nodded at me. "Whut up, big homie? You know I got that bread for you," he said, pulling out a fat as knot of hundreds. He peeled me off fifty of them.

I took them bitches and put 'em in my pocket. Now, I was open to listening to him. "How you niggas link up?" I asked, wanting them to fill in the blanks of everything that I had missed since I had been missing in action for a few days.

Nut blew the smoke out and grabbed an apple juice off of the night table. "I fuck with Sun. Every time I come down here, Nikki be fuckin' off with his sister, Tameka, so me and the lil' homie got acquainted. He be showing me around the city and shit. Anyway, I saw lil' fam going into a gas station over on Roosevelt Avenue and I told him jump in. Then, I had to pick his brain. That's when I found out that he work for Sherm. He told me that word was out that Sherm put the hit on Nikki's crib because of that Bryan nigga. Not only that, I guess that other nigga Mickey still hanging on to dear life over at Mount Sinai. Kid in and out, but every time he come in, he running his mouth."

Tim nodded. "Yeah, and he saying that Nikki's right hand man, which is you, shot him up and snuffed his patna at his baby momma crib. Sherm put ten bands on yo' head for the first nigga to bring you to him alive, and five if a nigga just kill you. I know that's peanuts, but everybody know that if they do a favor for Sherm, you got the go ahead to eat in Cloverland, so it's ain't about the immediate money, it's about the long-term benefit."

Nut pulled off of the blunt. "Only good thing is don't nobody know where you stay, or who you really are, other than a few. I advise we go bag this nigga, and get this shit over with. That way, we avenge Nikki and we take out an enemy at the same time."

The details were so vague that it was kind of throwing me for a loop. I knew that I needed to ask so many questions, but in my opinion, I knew that it would only waste time. I felt like we needed to get at this nigga's chin and get shit over with. I was turning eighteen in a few days and I needed for all of this stuff to be behind me. "Aiight, then. So, you sure you can get us in this nigga's tip? What makes you so sure?" I asked, sitting on the bed and feeling my stomach turn into butterflies.

I didn't know why I was feeling so uneasy. Maybe because of the fact that I knew we was about to get into some real live drama while hanging on the word of a lil' nigga that I barely trusted. Or maybe it was the fact that I was so close to being eighteen that it felt like something bad was gon' happen before I was able to make it all the way there. Whatever it was, I was ready to move and get it over with. I felt that with Sherm putting money on my head, it was gon' give me more enemies than I could handle. So. the best thing to do was to whack that nigga.

Tim grabbed a .45 off of the bed and cocked it back. "Hell yeah, I can get y'all in. That nigga trust me, and he think I'm scared of him, but I ain't. I ain't scared of no nigga. The worst thing that can happen to me is death, and I ain't scared to die. I just don't give a fuck, ever since my mother got killed." He frowned.

I already knew how the game went. If that nigga Sherm was putting up ten gees on my head, then I had to offer the lil' homie slightly more than that, or it just wouldn't make sense. At that time, he didn't owe me no loyalty, and I didn't expect it from him. But I had to pull things in my favor. I had to play a few mental games with him. If I didn't, it could cost me my life.

I went into my pocket and pulled back out the five stacks that he had given me, and handed it to him. "Here, lil' homie. This you for being so stomp down. I got ten more at the crib that's yours. That'll give you fifteen total. I'm also gon' put some work in yo' hand that'll be yours. You don't owe me shit, other than yo' loyalty. Let's seal this shit in blood, lil' nigga."

Tim took the money and looked me up and down, then shook his head. "N'all, it ain't even about the dough, Blood. I remember you put that work in my hand, way before this nigga Sherm forced me to work for him. I honor you, man, and that's all that's to it. Now, once you knock this nigga off and the west side of Cloverland open up, why don't you give me a slot in yo' crew. Not as no petty hustler, either. I'm talking a slot where I'll be able to have lil' niggas run under me. I got a few project kids that's out here starving. Niggas that's so grimy that won't nobody fuck with 'em, but I trust 'em. I know they'll eat with me on some loyalty shit. All I need is the plug and the go ahead," he said, putting his pistol into the small of his back.

I was starting to like lil' homie more and more. I nodded and started to envision everything that he was saying. If I chose to step out into the slums like that, I would love to have a crew of young, hungry goons behind me that was about that life. "I'll tell you what, lil' homie. You set this shit up the right way and we'll make this shit happen. I'll make sure that you and all of yo' lil' homies eat good. Nigga, we'll eat off of the same plate. That's on my mother, may she rest in peace." I had to slip that last part in there to let him know that my mother was gone too. I felt like it would draw him closer to me, and that's what I needed during this time.

He nodded furiously. "That's what I'm talking about. Look, that nigga Sherm supposed to be throwing a skating birthday party for his daughter on Saturday for her thirteenth birthday. He and his baby momma, Shondra, having it at Skate University off of the highway. It's from six until midnight. That fool gon' have a few niggas with him, but for the most part, his defenses gon' be lowered. That'll be the best time to body his ass, and I'll even buss this gun for you to prove my loyalty. I ain't no lil' kid no more. I'ma show you that. Just let me make sure everything is still everything, and I'ma get back to you, ASAP. That's my word." He leaned forward and gave me a half hug.

I hugged him for a brief second, and then pat him on the back. "Fuck with me and we gon' eat my nigga. Loyalty over everything. Live and die by that shit. You hear me?"

He nodded. "Loud and clear."

After I left them, I texted Purity and told her to meet me around the corner from the Deacon's crib. My mother was set to have a sit down with them that Sunday, and I just wanted to see Purity in the physical before all of that took place. I missed her, and I wanted to hug my lil' sister.

The sun was just going behind the clouds when I saw her round the corner, and jog to my car. I opened the door and met her half way, scooping her into the air while she wrapped her arms and legs around me, holding me tight.

"I missed you so much, Shemar. I hate when you stay away from me for so long. It makes me so weak." She hugged me tighter, then I let her down on to her feet.

I took her beautiful face into my hands and rubbed her tears away with my thumbs. "I missed you too, baby sis, and I be thinking about you every second when I'm not with you. You should already know that. I gotta get things right for you. I gotta get you out of that house."

She lowered her head, and wrapped her arms around herself, avoiding any eye contact with me. She blinked and more tears fell down her cheeks, then she shook her head slowly. She opened her mouth to say something, but no words came out. Then, she turned her back to me altogether.

I grabbed her shoulder and made her face me. I looked her over real carefully. Still, she managed to avoid any eye contact with me. "Purity, what's the matter? Why are you refusing to look at me right now? Talk to me, lil' sis."

I tilted her head upward by using her chin. Tears dripped off of it, and I started to feel really sick. I could tell that something was wrong with her, and I needed to know.

Purity turned her back on me again, and started to walk away from me. "Shemar, don't worry about getting me from him anymore. I'm not even worth it. You should be focusing on going to college and not about my life and my well-being. I ain't nothing. Just a dope addict's daughter with no future. I'm lower than scum." She took off running, and it took me a while to process everything that she had said.

I stood there for a second longer, and then I took off after her. I caught her by the corner, wrapped her into my arms and picked her up, carrying her all the way to my car before I set her back down. "Get yo' ass in the car, Purity, and tell me what's going on. I'm not playin' with you, lil' sis."

She stomped her foot. "Why? I don't want you to know because you gon' hate me." Snot ran out of her nose as more tears dropped off of her chin. She looked like she was on the verge of breaking down to her knees.

I had only seen her like that one other time. That was when we had found out our parents were dead and we would be snatched up by the State of Texas. Now I knew that something had to be utterly wrong.

I came around and opened the car door. "Get in, Purity, right now!" I hollered, feeling a lump come into my throat. I was scared out of my mind and I didn't even know why.

She got into the car, and I slammed the door after her leg disappeared inside of the vehicle.

After she was in, I ran around the car, got in myself and locked the doors. "Now, tell me what the matter is."

She shook her head. "Shemar, don't you understand that you are all that I have, and that if you hate me then I am going to hate myself even worse than I already do?" she asked with her voice breaking up horribly. She started to shake. Snot came out of her nostrils, and she sniffed it back into her nose and swallowed.

I grabbed her hand as I felt myself getting choked up. This was my little sister and I could tell that she was in dire pain. She needed me. She felt for some reason that I would turn my back on her when that would never be the case. I just wanted to know what the matter was so I could heal her. So I could protect her as best as I could.

I picked up her hand and kissed the back of it, then opened the palm and placed it against my face. "Purity, you are my everything, baby. I would never leave you nor forsake you. It is my job to protect you, and I will die doing that. Please, tell me what is going on. I need to know. I am beggin' you." I cried.

She shook her head, then dropped her face into her lap, before tilting her head back and sniffing her snot back into her nose again. "I'm pregnant, Shemar. I'm pregnant, and I don't know if it's by the Deacon or his oldest son, Mark, because both of them have been raping me for the last few months." She lowered her face back into her lap and started to bawl so loud that I started crying.

I was broken, lost and confused. I sat there for a long time, not knowing what to say, but with murder definitely on my mind. I knew I would kill them. I knew I would kill the whole family. Even the mother, if I had to, because they had hurt my little sister in the worst way known to man.

"Say something, Shemar! You're making me feel so, so, badddd," she cried, rocking back and forth. She broke into a fit of coughs and then got to gagging.

I felt like I was hurting her because I didn't know what to say. All I saw was red. I wanted to kill every nigga on earth over her. I was shaking so bad that my teeth started chattering loudly as if I were cold.

Finally, I snapped out of it and wrapped my arm around her. "Purity, I'm so sorry that you had to go through that, lil' sister, but I can promise you that you won't ever have to go through that shit ever again. You know I'm finna kill them. All of them muhfuckas. Don't nobody hurt my lil' sister! Nobody! You are my angel. You are precious! You are my absolute guiding light in this world of darkness, and I will never let you reach harm again, as long as I am alive. I promise." I pulled her into my embrace, and held her while we both cried against each other.

After a half hour of that, she found her voice. "Shemar, you know what? Even though I know it's a sin to kill people, I really want you to kill all of them, because they hurt me so bad. They hurt me so, so bad, big bruh, and I hate myself because of it." She laid her head on my shoulder while I imagined how I was going to kill them.

I knew I wouldn't be able to sleep until I completed that task. I had to put the pieces of the puzzle together, but when it was all said and done, they were going to pay for hurting my lil' sister.

"What about Candace, the mother? Did she ever hurt you in anyway?" I asked, trying to see if I needed to body her as well.

She shook her head. "I know she knew, but she had never laid a finger on me. Do I have to go back there tonight? And what am I gon' do about this baby? I don't know if I wanna keep it or not."

I shook my head. "You gotta go back there tonight, sis, but before anybody can bother you, I'll be there, taking care of business. You already know

I ain't finna play about you. Now, these sick ass people been violating you for the longest, and it breaks my heart that this is the first time that I'm hearing about it. Can you tell me why that is? Why you didn't feel you could come to me? I thought that we were each other's worlds?" I was feeling sicker and sicker the more it set in that my lil' sister had actually been violated by these people. The more I looked at her and noticed how vulnerable she really was, and the fact that she was carrying one of their children, it was starting to break me up inside. I was trying my best to put on a brave face for her, but deep within the pits f my soul I was crying like a new born baby, and felt sicker than a person with pneumonia.

Purity shrugged and exhaled loudly. "Shemar, you are my world, and I know I should have told you earlier, but I just didn't know how to. I thought that you would look at me like I was a hoe or something, or like it was my fault that they were going in on me. After the Deacon took my virginity, I didn't feel like your little angel anymore. I felt like a harlot, and lower than scum. I thought that after you found out, you wouldn't see me in the same light. I mean, why wouldn't you?" She lowered her head back into her lap before covering it with her face. "I'm too young for all of this shit to happen to me. All I want is to live with you. Is that so much to ask?" she whimpered.

I rubbed her back and tried to keep the tears from falling from my eyes. A man never knew how much he could really take until he was in the position that I was in. No matter what had happened to her, I was still seeing her as my little baby sister. Almost like as if she were still a toddler and trying to walk. Every time I imagined them forcing themselves on her, or making my lil' sister cry, I wanted to kill them right in that moment, but I knew I had to be smart, even though the urges were getting the better of me. I look back on everything right now and I see that it was the situation with Purity and the Deacon's family that turned me into a cold-hearted savage.

I placed Purity's face in my hands and looked into her eyes. "From now on, if ever anyone or anything is hurting you, you come to me about it right away, because I am your protector, and it's my job to be there for you against all odds. You are still my angel, and I love you even more. I will never stop. Do you understand me?"

She nodded, then closed her eyes as I kissed her on the forehead, afterward hugging her close to my heart for the next hour. Before she got out of my car, we came up with a plan that would seal the Deacon and Mark's fate.

Ghost

Chapter 16

I sat in my car for a long time, just thinking after Purity had gotten out of it. I could still smell my sister's perfume in the air. I missed her already, and I was trying my best to not feel like such a failure for not being there for her when she really needed me to be. I mean, I knew that the way things were set up, it would have been nearly impossible for me to have been able to prevent them, but you couldn't tell my mind that. All I saw was my wounded baby sister that needed me to save her, and I was willing to do anything that I had too in order to save her.

I went home and got about two hours of sleep, because I was so exhausted that I couldn't even think straight. I needed some mental strength, and I would need it in order to carry out my next order of business.

Purity said that the Deacon had a habit of coming into her room every night after he got home from his grave digging job at three in the morning. She said he had this habit where he would shower, then warm up his food that Candace had cooked for him, eat half of it, then come into her room and have his way with her until he was finished. Then, he'd go and finish his meal before getting into the bed with his wife. She said that all of this would start between three in the morning and three thirty. So, I set my alarm for two thirty, and I woke up before it even went off, got dressed, and loaded up with everything that I was gon' need to handle my business.

I locked the door to my room just in case my mother or Simone tried to come in and they'd discover that I wasn't in the bed. I mean, it wasn't that big of a deal, I was just trying to cover all of my bases. So, I locked the door and hopped out of my bedroom window, crept alongside of the house until I got to the backyard, hopped the fence and wound up in the dark alley as the rain fell from the sky in a drizzle. I guessed that since it was April, Houston was going through its rainy season, and I was already tired of it.

I took the alley about ten houses down as one dog barked at me after the next. That shit was getting on my nerves because I was hoping that they didn't wake the Robinson family up before I got there. Luckily, that wasn't the case.

When I got to the back of their yard, I hopped the tall fence, and landed on both feet under the cover of darkness. Then, I jogged to the side of it and paused under Purity's window. I was just about to stand on my tippy toes and tap on the glass when she opened it, and stuck her head out of it.

She put her finger to her lip. "Shhh. Candace just went to sleep after drinking a half bottle of Korbel. I think she gon' be out for a minute. Mark here, but his brothers staying with their grandmother for the weekend. He just tapped on my door and said that he was finna be back, so I guess that mean he finna try me before his daddy get home, like he do on most nights. Please, don't let him, Shemar. I'm begging you. I can't take them being in my body again." She looked like she was about to become hysterical.

I waved her out of the way. "Watch out. I'm coming in there."

The look on her face was all I needed to see to unleash that cold heart of mine. I was finna make a statement to every rapist, pedophile muhfucka in the world. I was thinking about doing some things to them that I had never done before.

I tossed my bag into the window and then jumped and climbed into until I fell onto Purity's carpet. She was looking at the door like she was scared out of her mind. I even peeped that her knees were knocking into each other.

She put a finger into her mouth and bit on the nail. "Shemar. I'm so scared. Please tell me that everything is going to be alright," she whimpered in a shaky voice.

I stood up and pulled her to me, hugged her real quick, kissed her on the cheek, then held her face again. "Look, I got this. We ride for each other. Our loyalty is in blood. They will never hurt you again. Just get back in your bed and get under the covers. Don't move until I give you the signal that we discussed, then you gon' jump out of the window and go call the police, telling them that somebody robbing the house. That's after I fuck this Deacon over. You got that?"

She nodded, getting back into the bed and pulling the covers up to her chin. I could see that she was still shaking and worried, but I couldn't focus on that right then.

"Sis, where is Mark's room?" I asked, kneeling and pulling out an eight-inch hunting knife that the Pastor had bought me for my fourteeth birthday. During that age, he took me hunting for deer every winter, and I loved it.

She pointed with her thumb. "His room is the first room to your right, at the top of the stairs. I heard the shower running a lil' while ago, which means that he's probably showering and preparing to get ready for me. He always goes to his room to get dressed. You'll catch him there."

That was all I needed to hear. I kissed Purity on the forehead, then made my way to the staircase. Once there, I looked up them, then ascended the stairs, looking behind me into the dark house. It was relatively quiet with the exception of the stairs squeaking every so often. My heart was beating fast because I wanted to hurry up and kill Mark before the Deacon got home. I didn't want to waste too much time with him because I wanted to savor the Deacon's murder. A grown ass man, hopping on top of my sister, just wasn't sitting right with me. He had stolen her innocence and I was gon' make him pay for that.

As I got to the top of the stairs, I heard the water still going inside of the bathroom. I looked to my right and saw that Mark's room door was opened. I stepped inside of it. He had a fresh pair of boxers laid out on the bed, along with a white beater and ankle socks. On his stereo was the sounds of Bruno Mars. Just as I stepped all the way inside of his room, I heard the water in the bathroom shut off, then seconds later, the door was opening up.

My heart beat faster in my chest. I hid behind the door and took a deep breath. Then, I slid my ski mask all the way down my face now, after wearing it as a hat until that time.

As soon as Mark stepped into the room, he kicked the door closed behind him and started to singing along to the song that was coming out of the speakers. But then, his eyes grew as big as hell when he saw me. Before he could even utter a word, I ran forward and stabbed him right at the top of his collar bone, and ripped the blade to the right, before pulling it out.

Blood skeeted across his shoulder. He grabbed his neck with two hands and fell to his knees with his blood seeping through his fingers. He tried to talk, but no sound came out of his mouth; only blood.

I kneeled beside him while he scooted backward on his ass to get away from me. The digital clock on his dresser read 2:55AM. "You bitch ass rapist," I whispered. "How dare you and yo' sick ass father assault my sister? You muhfuckas must've thought it was sweet or somethin', huh?" I took my mask off and sat it on his bed. I wanted this bitch ass nigga to see my face. I hated rapists like him. I still do to this day.

He shook his head from left to right, and kept scooting backward until his back parked up against the wall under his bedroom window. Once again, he tried to talk, but only managed to gurgle on his own blood.

I got closer to him, slammed the knife into his chest, and pulled downward, slicing him open and leaving a thick gash that spilled his plasma. He started to holler only loud enough for me to hear him. The blood in his throat blocked him from getting any louder.

I grabbed him by the neck, took the knife and swished it through the air until the blade cut into his face again and again, while he struggled against me to no avail. He yelped like a dog being kicked in the balls, and I felt no regard for him. I was thinking about how ugly he made my sister feel. How he helped to ruin her for the moment. How he forced his seed into her body, and destroyed her self-image. I saw her face in my mind, full of tears. Her heart full of pain and agony, all because of him and the sick ass Deacon. I slashed him across the face again and again, over and over, watching his blood shoot everywhere.

Finally, after I could barely breathe, I reached between his legs, grabbed his lil' dick, and sawed it off, before stuffing it into his mouth. Then, I rolled his punk ass under his bed, put my mask back on, grabbed all of my shit, and made my way out of his room and back to Purity's.

As soon as I opened her door she jumped up in bed, looking fearful. I put my finger to my lip. "Be cool, sis, it's just me," I whispered, closing her door behind me.

She hopped out of the bed and wrapped her arms around me. "I'm so scared, Shemar. I don't know what to do. I'm in here freaking out. Did you get him already?" she asked, looking up at me with her big eyes.

I nodded. "Yeah. Dude out for the count. You ain't gotta worry about him no more. Now I'm finna take a good look at this Deacon. After that, you gon' be home-free. I'll never let you be harmed again. I promise."

She hugged me really tight, and laid her head on my chest. "I love you so much, big bruh. I can't wait to live with you every day, for the rest of my life. I'm so tired of being scared all the time."

Just as she said this, I could hear the Deacon's truck pulling into the driveway. I knew it was his, because, for one, it was three in the morning on the dot. Two, he had these loud ass pipes on his truck that gave him away.

I could feel Purity start to shake real bad in my arms. "That's him, Shemar. He's here, and he finna come and get me. I just know he is." She hugged me with all of her might.

I pulled her arms from around my waist and looked down on her. "Listen to me. I want you to just chill for a minute. Get back in your bed, and I'ma hide in this closet. When he come in here, I'm gon' take care of him. I promise you that. Don't trip. Just trust me."

By this time, she was shaking so bad that she could barely stand up. Seeing her like that was making me feel sick on the stomach. It was also making me hate the Deacon even more. I felt like he had ruined my sister on so many levels. Him and his dead ass son.

"Just trust me, Purity. Get back in the bed." I lead her to the bed and put the blankets back over her, while she laid on her back, reluctantly.

Grabbing all of my things, I shimmied into her closet and left it open, just a peek. My heart was once again beating fast. I wanted to get this last task done and over with. At that time, I didn't know if I was going to kill Candace along with her husband and son, but it wasn't off of the table.

Almost like clockwork, as soon as the Deacon closed the front door, no less than a minute later he was at Purity's bedroom door. He knocked once, and then opened her door and walked in, smelling like death and dirt. "Hey, baby girl, are you awake down there?" he asked, before sitting on the edge of her bed. He pulled the cover back some to expose her face more.

I noted that Purity jerked in the bed.

His face scrunched as if he was going to hit her.

"Yes, I'm awake, but I'm sleepy. I don't want to do anything tonight. Please, don't make me," she whined, and scooted away from him.

While I didn't want to put my sister through that bullshit that he was about to try and take her through, I still wanted to see for myself how he got down on her when nobody else was around. I guess I just needed to make my heart even more cold in that moment.

He shook his head. "Now, now, baby girl. I done already told you that you never deny me of anything. Whenever the Deacon wants some of his baby girl, he gets it. That's the whole reason I adopted you. Don't try and act like you don't be wanting me too. If I recall, you be getting wetter than a hurricane for yo' old man, down there." He smiled, and put his hand under her covers.

My sister jerked, then started to whimper while his hand moved around a lot.

That was all that I could take. I rushed out of the closet and pressed my .45 to his cheek. "You sick ass bitch nigga, get you muthafucking hands out of her covers and stand yo' punk ass up." I jammed the barrel more firm into his cheek, and grabbed him by the back of the neck, forcing him upward.

He stood and put his hands in the air. "Shemar, now, I know that's you. You don't have to do this. Me and your sister was just playing. I wasn't gon' touch her fa real. Honest."

I wrapped my arm under his throat and squeezed. Not enough to choke him, but enough to let him know that I was serious. "Purity, now, go. Wait ten minutes, then make that call. Go now, ma."

I waited until she grabbed her phone and a pair of shoes. Then, she jumped out of her bedroom window. My phone buzzed while I had my arm wrapped around his neck with my chest to his back. I tightened my grip, choking him some, and without him knowing, looked at the face of my phone. It was a text from my mother, telling me that Nikki was out of her coma and was crying to see me. My heart skipped a beat. I imagined Nikki's face, worried and alone, wondering where I was. It made me feel some type of way because I wanted to be there when she opened her eyes.

The Deacon struggled against me, and I could feel his saliva on my arm. "Ack. Ack. Shemar, I—" That was all he was able to get out before I tossed him onto the bed and pointed my gun at him.

I knew that time was of the essence; that Purity was going to be calling the police in any minute, and due to the fact that we stayed in a middle-class neighborhood, it wasn't going to take them long to get there.

"You rapist ass bitch. I knew you was going in on my sister. Now yo' punk ass gon' pay. I leaned forward and cracked him across the forehead with the handle of my .45, opening him up. *Bam!*

He jerked backward, with blood pouring out of him right away. Before he could get used to that blow, I slammed it into him Again, in damn near the same spot. *Bam!*

He flew backward and threw his arms up. "Shemar, you don't have to do this, man! I'm sorry! I'll never touch her again! I swear to it! Please believe me!" He hollered so loud that I was worried he was gon' wake up the neighbors.

I wasn't trying to hear none of that shit. I had my mind on beating him to death and making him pay for everything that he and his son had done to my sister. He deserved a painful death. All rapists did, in my opinion. So, I reached back and slammed the handle into his face again, cracking him above the eye. I went to pull the gun back, but he grabbed my arm, before jumping his fat ass on top of me.

"Give me this gun, little boy. I said I was sorry. Haven't you ever heard of forgiveness?" His fat fingers struggled to get the gun out of my hand, and I struggled to keep it.

I knew that if he got that gun away from me that I was a dead man, either by him, or by the police when they found Mark's body in the other room. I started to panic, and I became short of breath.

We continued to tussle with the gun, back and forth, so much so that we fell to the floor, with me on top of him, still trying to get the gun out of his grasp. More than once the barrel was pointed at me, so I had to redirect it from fear of it going off and a bullet slamming into my face. He pulled our arms upward with the gun held above our heads. We continued to struggle, breathing hard, and wrestling without using our arms because all four of our hands were wrapped around the pistol.

Finally, after seeing that I wasn't going to get it away from him, I leaned forward and bit him right on his fat ass cheek. I got a whole mouth full too, before biting down, and pulling with all of my might. *Chomp!*

His eyes got so big that the skin on his forehead wrinkled up. Then, he was hollering at the top of his lungs. "Arrrgggghhh!"

I felt his blood spurt into my mouth, and that didn't stop me from pulling his cheek right off of his face and spitting it on the carpet. Before I could think about it, I chomped down on his left cheek and did the same thing, but this time I bit into him so deep that my teeth rubbed against his cheekbone. It felt gritty.

He started to kick his legs. Just as I thought, he let the gun go, and I stood up with it, aiming it down at him. I tasted his blood on my tongue and it only excited me more. Now, I was ready to kill this predator. This sicko, this poor excuse of a man, for my sister and a million other females that had to endure some of the similar things that he'd imposed on them.

I looked down on him with the two big, bloody holes in his face. I could see his bone underneath where his cheek had once been. Blood gushed out of the wounds as he struggled to get up. He looked exhausted.

I smacked him with the pistol again, right against his temple. knocking him on to his back. *Bam!* "Bitch ass nigga. That's what you get." *Bam!*

He turned on his side and drug himself across the carpet. "I'm sorry, Shemar. Please don't do this. Please, don't take my life. I'm only human. I didn't mean to hurt your sister. I swear I didn't." He turned over until he was facing me, laying on his back with a pool of blood on the front of his gray uniform.

I aimed at his forehead, ready to pull the trigger when I thought about how loud the blast would be. It would surely wake the neighbors, and anybody else that was sleeping in the house, including a drunk Candace. I couldn't take that chance. I had to get out of there without making a major mistake. The police had to be on their way by now.

I kicked him with all of my might, right between his legs, and watched him curl into a ball. Then, I put the .45 back into the small of my back. I jogged over to my bag and pulled back out the hunting knife before straddling him. "Don't nobody put they hands on my sister. That's my heart right there, and this shit sealed in blood!" I slammed the knife downward, but before it could make contact with this fat ass nigga, he bucked his hips and threw me into the dresser, hard.

I slammed my head against the pink wood and almost lost consciousness. Through foggy eyes, I watched the Deacon climb to his feet and make his way toward the bedroom door.

He threw it open, and staggered into the living room. "Candy! Candy! Baby, help me! Help me, baby!" he hollered.

I slowly got up, feeling nausea set into me. I used the dresser as a crutch to get to my feet. I stumbled for a few steps. Then, I took off running as fast as I could, raising the knife over my head, and slamming it into the Deacon's back. It felt like I was stabbing a mattress. The point must've crashed into his bone or something.

"Ahhhh! Shit!" He crashed into the dining room table, and fell on top of it. It made so much noise that I became beyond paranoid.

I felt my phone buzz again in my pocket, and that made me think of Nikki. I had to get to her after making sure that Purity was okay. I needed to kill the Deacon and get the fuck out of his house before the cops got there first.

I pulled the knife downward, shredding apart his back. His gray uniform tore and filled with blood. I pulled the knife out of his back just to slam it into him again. "Die, muthafucka! Damn!" I said, getting frustrated with his will to live.

He picked up the table and threw it out of the way, turned around and tackled me to the floor with the blade still in his back.

I felt him wrap his hand around my neck. "Uh! Uh! You little Satan. Die, Satan. Get thee behind me!" he hollered, slobbering at the mouth.

I twisted this way and that as the blood from his cheeks dripped onto my face. With all of my might, I humped upward, bucking him off of me just enough to pull the knife out of his back. Then, I jumped to my feet and attacked him again, slamming it into his chest as he tried to get up, right in the right side.

His eyes opened wider. He fell to one knee and looked me in the face with blood pouring out of his mouth, shaking like it was below zero in the room.

I pushed it more into him, and twisted the blade.

"Awww!" He groaned, holding my hand.

I pulled the knife out of him, ready to slam it back in, when I heard her voice. "Baby, where are you! Where are you?" Candace hollered from somewhere upstairs.

I took one look toward the steps, and that was all it took for the Deacon to head-butt me, knocking me back, before making his way toward the stairs.

"I'm down here, Candy! Help me! Shemar's killing me!"

Getting head-butted gotta be the worst pain known to man, or at least in the top three. I was so blessed that he didn't head -butt me in the nose because he would have broken my shit. He just caught me in the left eye, but it was enough to let me know that that shit was no joke.

I recovered quickly though, shook off the assault and met his ass before he could get to the second stair. That's where I raised the knife over my head and brought it down, fast and hard. *Bam!* Afterward, I pulled it out, slamming it into him all over again with hatred. I got to stabbing him so many times that I lost count. I just went nuts— stabbing, and shredding, then stabbing some more while he groaned underneath me. I imagined he was too weak to crawl.

He turned over onto his back and tried to grab the knife away from me. Blood was everywhere. All over the floor, the stairs, and our clothes. I looked like I had been playing in burgundy paint all day. There was also the smell of it in the air.

Candace came to the top of the staircase, looking down on us, wearing nothing but her robe. "Hey! Leave him alone! You're fuckin' killing my husband!" She made her way down the stairs, then stopped half way and took off running back up them, before she disappeared down the long hallway up there.

I was in my own zone. I was looking the Deacon in his eyes while I stabbed him again and again. The blade went in and out of his body, stabbing his torso to shreds. Then, I got to attacking his face with the blade, thinking about my lil' sister and all of the pain that she had to go through at his hands. I wanted to kill him more and more for killing and stealing her innocence.

I came out of my zone when my phone buzzed, nearly scaring me to death. Then, I heard a loud ass *chick-chick!* I looked up the stairs to see Candace holding a big, double barrel shotgun.

"You killed him! You killed my husband!" She ran down the stairs, just as I turned to run in the other direction.

I could hear the sirens of the police as they slammed on their brakes in front of the house, and then she shot to kill.

Boooommm!

To Be Continued...
Bred by the Slums 2
Coming Soon

Stay Connected with Us!

Text **LOCKDOWN** to 22828 to stay
up-to-date with new releases, sneak peaks,
contests and more…

Thank you!

Coming Soon from Lock Down Publications/Ca$h Presents

BOW DOWN TO MY GANGSTA

By **Ca$h**

TORN BETWEEN TWO

By **Coffee**

BLOOD STAINS OF A SHOTTA **II**

By **Jamaica**

WHEN THE STREETS CLAP BACK **II**

By **Jibril Williams**

STEADY MOBBIN

By **Marcellus Allen**

BLOOD OF A BOSS **V**

By **Askari**

BRIDE OF A HUSTLA **III**

By **Destiny Skai**

WHEN A GOOD GIRL GOES BAD **II**

By **Adrienne**

LOVE & CHASIN' PAPER **II**

By **Qay Crockett**

THE HEART OF A GANGSTA **III**

By **Jerry Jackson**

LOYAL TO THE GAME **IV**

LOVE ME WHEN IT HURTS

By **T.J. & Jelissa**

Ghost

A DOPEBOY'S PRAYER **II**

By **Eddie "Wolf" Lee**

IF LOVING YOU IS WRONG... **III**

By **Jelissa**

BLOODY COMMAS **III**

SKI MASK CARTEL **II**

By **T.J. Edwards**

BLAST FOR ME **II**

RAISED AS A GOON **V**

BRED BY THE SLUMS **II**

By **Ghost**

A DISTINGUISHED THUG STOLE MY HEART **III**

By **Meesha**

ADDICTIED TO THE DRAMA **II**

By **Jamila Mathis**

LIPSTICK KILLAH **II**

By **Mimi**

THE BOSSMAN'S DAUGHTERS 4

By **Aryanna**

Available Now

RESTRAINING ORDER **I & II**

By **CA$H & Coffee**

LOVE KNOWS NO BOUNDARIES **I II & III**

By **Coffee**

RAISED AS A GOON I, II, III & IV

By **Ghost**

LAY IT DOWN **I & II**

LAST OF A DYING BREED

BLOOD STAINS OF A SHOTTA

By **Jamaica**

LOYAL TO THE GAME

LOYAL TO THE GAME II

LOYAL TO THE GAME III

By **TJ & Jelissa**

BLOODY COMMAS I & II

SKI MASK CARTEL

By **T.J. Edwards**

IF LOVING HIM IS WRONG...I & II

By **Jelissa**

WHEN THE STREETS CLAP BACK

By **Jibril Williams**

A DISTINGUISHED THUG STOLE MY HEART I & II

By **Meesha**

PUSH IT TO THE LIMIT

By **Bre' Hayes**

BLOOD OF A BOSS **I, II, III & IV**

By **Askari**

THE STREETS BLEED MURDER **I, II & III**

THE HEART OF A GANGSTA I & II

Ghost

By **Jerry Jackson**

CUM FOR ME

CUM FOR ME 2

CUM FOR ME 3

An **LDP Erotica Collaboration**

BRIDE OF A HUSTLA **I & II**

THE FETTI GIRLS **I, II& III**

By **Destiny Skai**

WHEN A GOOD GIRL GOES BAD

By **Adrienne**

A GANGSTER'S REVENGE **I II III & IV**

THE BOSS MAN'S DAUGHTERS

THE BOSS MAN'S DAUGHTERS II

THE BOSSMAN'S DAUGHTERS III

A SAVAGE LOVE **I & II**

BAE BELONGS TO ME

A HUSTLER'S DECEIT I, II

By **Aryanna**

A KINGPIN'S AMBITON

A KINGPIN'S AMBITION **II**

I MURDER FOR THE DOUGH

By **Ambitious**

TRUE SAVAGE

TRUE SAVAGE II

TRUE SAVAGE **III**

Bred by the Slums

By **Chris Green**

A DOPEBOY'S PRAYER

By **Eddie "Wolf" Lee**

THE KING CARTEL **I, II & III**

By **Frank Gresham**

THESE NIGGAS AIN'T LOYAL **I, II & III**

By **Nikki Tee**

GANGSTA SHYT **I II &III**

By **CATO**

THE ULTIMATE BETRAYAL

By **Phoenix**

BOSS'N UP **I , II & III**

By **Royal Nicole**

I LOVE YOU TO DEATH

By Destiny J

I RIDE FOR MY HITTA

I STILL RIDE FOR MY HITTA

By **Misty Holt**

LOVE & CHASIN' PAPER

By **Qay Crockett**

TO DIE IN VAIN

By **ASAD**

BROOKLYN HUSTLAZ

By **Boogsy Morina**

BROOKLYN ON LOCK I & II

Ghost

By **Sonovia**

GANGSTA CITY

By **Teddy Duke**

A DRUG KING AND HIS DIAMOND

A DOPEMAN'S RICHES

By Nicole Goosby

BOOKS BY LDP'S CEO, CA$H

TRUST IN NO MAN

TRUST IN NO MAN 2

TRUST IN NO MAN 3

BONDED BY BLOOD

SHORTY GOT A THUG

THUGS CRY

THUGS CRY 2

THUGS CRY 3

TRUST NO BITCH

TRUST NO BITCH 2

TRUST NO BITCH 3

TIL MY CASKET DROPS

RESTRAINING ORDER

RESTRAINING ORDER 2

IN LOVE WITH A CONVICT

Coming Soon

BONDED BY BLOOD 2

BOW DOWN TO MY GANGSTA

Ghost

Printed in the USA
CPSIA information can be obtained
at www.ICGtesting.com
CBHW051226200124
3632CB00011B/790